# The Worlds We Leave Behind

# Books by A.F. Harrold

*The Imaginary*
Illustrated by Emily Gravett

*The Afterwards*
Illustrated by Emily Gravett

*The Song from Somewhere Else*
Illustrated by Levi Pinfold

*The Worlds We Leave Behind*
Illustrated by Levi Pinfold

*The Book of Not Entirely Useful Advice*
Illustrated by Mini Grey

FOR SLIGHTLY YOUNGER READERS

The Greta Zargo books
Illustrated by Joe Todd-Stanton

The Fizzlebert Stump series
Illustrated by Sarah Horne

# The Worlds We Leave Behind

**A.F. Harrold**

*Illustrated by* **Levi Pinfold**

BLOOMSBURY
CHILDREN'S BOOKS
LONDON  OXFORD  NEW YORK  NEW DELHI  SYDNEY

BLOOMSBURY CHILDREN'S BOOKS
Bloomsbury Publishing Plc
50 Bedford Square, London WC1B 3DP, UK
29 Earlsfort Terrace, Dublin 2, Ireland

BLOOMSBURY, BLOOMSBURY CHILDREN'S BOOKS and the Diana logo
are trademarks of Bloomsbury Publishing Plc

First published in Great Britain in 2022 by Bloomsbury Publishing Plc

A catalogue record for this book is available from the British Library

ISBN: HB: 978-1-5266-2388-1; eBook: 978-1-5266-2384-3

2 4 6 8 10 9 7 5 3 1

Printed and bound in China by C&C Offset Printing Co. Ltd, Shenzhen, Guangdong

To find out more about our authors and books visit www.bloomsbury.com
and sign up for our newsletters

For Michael Groom, Alex Bell and James Heywood –
*for the wild woods we knew back then*
A.F. HARROLD

For Isaac
LEVI PINFOLD

# CONTENTS

# Some Are Born

Some are born to peace and joy
And some are born to sorrow
But only for a day as we
Shall not be here tomorrow.

Stevie Smith
from The Collected Poems
& Drawings of Stevie Smith
(Faber, 2015)

# MONDAY

Hex wasn't entirely sure how the girl had come to be hurt.

That morning he and Tommo had got on their bikes and they'd headed over the level crossing and down the hill, down to the woods.

On a map, the woods were a fat finger pointing away from town.

A brook ran through the middle and the trees formed a strip, a couple of hundred metres wide on either side, but dwindling and narrowing, closing in and petering out the further you went. Beyond them, on the left, was the road that led off to the next town. Beyond them, on the right, were wide, flat farmer's fields.

It wasn't big enough to get lost in, but it *was* big enough to forget yourself in.

The trees towered over you, little specks of blue twinkling high above like stars in the night sky, saying nothing.

As smoke and squeals had poured off Hex and Tommo's brake pads at the bottom of the last road, they had seen the girl in her front garden.

She was some years younger than they were. Down the bottom of the school, probably still in the infants, while they were up at the top.

She was called Sascha Something-or-Other and had been sat on the lawn of her front garden pretending to read from a book to her toys. ('Pretending' only because Hex couldn't believe the story was actually in the book, which looked like one about tractors.)

'There was a prince who killed a giant,' the girl had said, 'and he got sent to prison because killing is wrong, and when he was in prison he fell in love with the prison boss's daughter, but she wouldn't marry him because he had killed a giant and killing is wrong. But he said, "The giant was going to eat the king," and she said, "The king should be more careful." And she married an apple and ate it all up and was happily ever after. The end.'

The front door had been open a crack and they'd heard

distant voices somewhere inside.

She'd lowered her book and looked at them, squinting at the sun and shading her eyes with a hand.

'Whatcha doing?' she'd asked.

'Nothing,' they'd said.

But she'd asked again and so they'd told her they were going into the woods. There was a rope-swing set up on the high bank, over the brook. It was a good place to spend a hot day.

'I'll come,' she'd said, putting a plastic horse between the pages of her book and laying it down carefully on the grass.

'Nah,' they'd said.

But she'd just stood up and brushed her bottom with both hands.

She'd sniffed her palms and said, 'Mmmm, don't you love that fresh smell?'

She'd probably meant the grass, but it was still weird.

Tommo and Hex had looked at one another at that point. A half-chuckle, nervous and uncertain.

'Nah, you're OK,' they'd said, shaking their heads.

Pulling their bikes up they'd walked off, not looking back.

And she had followed them.

They hadn't invited her, hadn't forced her, hadn't encouraged her, hadn't *wanted* her to come, but there she was, a little kid suddenly in their care.

And now they were in the woods and it had all gone wrong.

❧

Hex often wondered why adults insisted on there being *reasons* for things.

That didn't match the world he saw.

Sometimes he'd stand up in class, in the middle of doing something else, and point at a squirrel out the window or do a little dance or ask a question about something they *weren't* studying that day, and the other kids would laugh, and Miss Short, his teacher (or, ten minutes later, Mr Dedman, the head), would look him in the eyes and say, 'What on earth did you do that for, Hector?'

And he'd shrug and say, 'I dunno,' and they'd tell him he was being smart and answering back, but he was simply telling the truth.

As he stood there, in front of the head's desk, sometimes an answer *would* come – something like 'Because I thought the squirrel was about to jump' – but these *reasons*, these *answers*, only ever came to him *after* the event, only when he was interrogated about it. They were never there in the moment.

And it seemed most of life was like that – you did things and then thought about why you'd done them later on, when someone asked, or when you got caught, or caught out.

Even with Tommo, they'd meet up each morning and just see where they ended up.

Today they'd ended up in the woods, with Sascha at their heels.

They'd walked their bikes down the twittern, the alley that ran between two houses at the end of the close, down to the edge of the woods.

There was a bin for dog owners and a sign that said the local council were being ever so generous by not selling the place off to build more houses. And there was a path in, under the trees. Well-trodden earth, made bare by feet, out of the sunshine, into the shade.

They'd been here a hundred times before, over the years, so they hadn't hesitated as they'd gone in, turning at all the right places, Tommo panting and rattling his inhaler as they climbed uphill, between trees, heading to the bank above the stream. With, to their almost-amusement, Sascha following, running round their ankles like a puppy, asking questions, laughing, singing.

Her eagerness had been embarrassing, and Hex had felt that embarrassment settle on him like a bird on his shoulder (it had almost looked like worry). It had pecked at his ear and said nothing.

Eventually they'd dumped their bikes on the ground.

There was a big tree, an oak, right on the edge, on the high lip of the riverbank. Its roots stuck out of the mud wall below, like rungs on a ladder.

From one of the high branches someone had tied a rope, a tatty thick blue nylon rope. And at the bottom of the rope was a crossbar, a sturdy stick held in place by a fat knot.

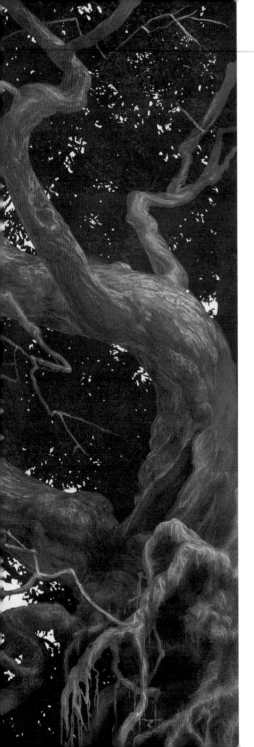

Below that, curling round at the base of the high bank, was the brook, a spotty dark mirror snaking through pale earth.

It hadn't rained for weeks, a long, dry spring after a sharp, cold winter, and the water was low. Pebbles poked dry heads into the air.

You could scramble down, using roots as footholds, and that's what Hex had done.

He'd got the crossbar in one hand (it had been at about head height), and had pulled it behind him as he climbed back up the bank.

At the top he'd cocked his leg over the wooden bar and, just as Tommo had shouted, 'Oi, I was gonna be first!' had pushed off.

'Geronimo!'

Sometimes Hex dreamt about flying.

He'd be running along the street or in the school field and he'd jump, just a normal jump, a hop-skip-and-a-jump sort of jump, and he'd stay up.

With a thought, with a push of his will, he'd rise a bit higher.

Not flying like a superhero, arm out in front, cloak flapping behind, but just like a boy who's jumped and decided not to come down yet.

And he'd steer, turn back and rise up higher, over his friends below, and look down on the black, tarmac-ish school roof, or at the tiled roofs of the houses, and will himself on, light and happy, between television aerials and on, up, out, over the town.

And that was all there was to the dream, that freedom and the feeling of joy, never an adventure,

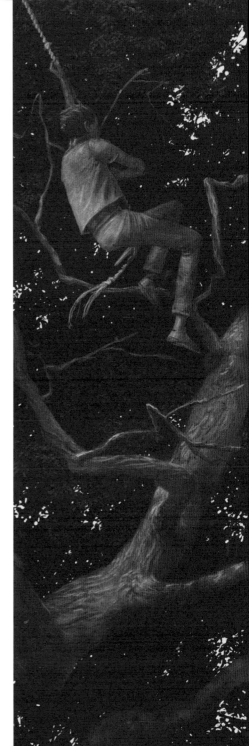

never a drama, never anyone shouting or wanting anything.

If the people below were pointing at him, if they were saying something, he never noticed – it was just him in the air with the wind in his hair, touching his toes on the crests of the roofs as he pushed off to sky-run some more.

But then, always, sooner or later, he'd wake up.

&

The rope-swing was the closest real life brought him to those dreams.

The freedom at the end of the upswing, as gravity forgot about you for a second or two ... before it called you back, and then the acceleration in the mouth of your stomach, fluttering as you zoomed down ... and through ... and up again ... the riverbank calling you back and then ... the pause, again, at the top, where you could reach out and step off ... but you don't, and you plunge back down again ... The speed, the speed, the joy.

(It was different to the feeling on the swings down the rec because of the coarse rope in his hands, the irregular, knobbly stick under his thighs, the organic creak and sway of the thick branch above, the green light of the trees all around, the *risk* of relying on some stranger's knots holding the whole experience together. It was like being a caveman, not a boy of the present with schoolwork and tests and a bedtime.)

He'd swung over the stream half a dozen times before Tommo had grabbed him, and they'd swapped places, and he'd watched his best friend close his eyes and grip the rope, and Hex had guessed how Tommo felt and had laughed again.

And then Sascha had said, 'My turn now.' And she'd bounced on her toes saying it, a stripped twig in her hands, which she waved like a magic wand, and her words became a command for the boys.

Hex had felt something in the world shift slightly to one side as he'd held the crossbar and Tommo had hoicked her up and helped her hook her legs over. First one, then the other.

They had held her there, in the air, by the great oak, her feet up off the ground, a vast open space before her, the stream below, the far-off trees on the other side, and just space, space, fresh air between here and there.

'You ready?' Hex had asked.

And for the first time there'd been something like nervousness in her eyes.

But he'd let go by then, just before Tommo did, and so she'd spun round and round as she'd swung out.

And she'd said nothing.

And the forest had said nothing.

And the brook below had said nothing.

And then Sascha had laughed and the silence went away as she pendulumed and pirouetted high up in the green woods.

She had tried to swing, to move like you do on a swing to go higher, to keep moving, but because she was spinning she sent the whole rope-swing round and round in crazy circles.

And the boys had laughed, because they'd just helped someone have fun and were Good People because of it.

And then … And then it had gone on a bit too long.

The rope-swing was settling down. She was now in control, no longer spinning so much. Swinging backwards and forwards, mostly, but not quite within reach of the bank. Slowing, despite her efforts.

And Hex had climbed down the root-ladder, down to the stream, and had tried to catch her as she went past, to drag her back over to the bank so she could climb off.

But she'd banged into him, by accident, knocking him on to his backside.

Water had soaked the seat of his jeans, giving him sudden, cold, damp underwear.

And up on the bank Tommo had laughed loudly, slapping the tree trunk, getting breathless, pointing down at him.

And Sasha was laughing too, looking down on him as the swing swung slowly back and forth.

It was a real crowd-in-the-playground moment – the world watching and you shrinking.

And Hex had felt microscopic.

Looking up into the canopy above he'd seen a squirrel jump

from one high branch to another, free-flying, landing, pausing, turning … its bead-like black eye watching him, deciding if he was a nut to store for winter.

And Hex was small.

Sascha was still swinging above him and she was singing as she swung, oblivious to the harm she'd done.

His heart hammered strange rhythms in his ears.

His cheeks burned.

And then, as he clambered up the low bank on the other side, his hand closed around a dry clod of mud. And as he stood he turned and he threw it.

It whizzed past Sascha, crumbling with a puff of dust on the opposite bank.

Her back was to him. She didn't see.

But Tommo did, and for whatever reason (for no good reason at all) he replied with a dirt-clod of his own.

The last few weeks had been dry, so the mud crumbled as it left your hands. Smoke trails in the air, explosive puffs as they hit the ground.

And Sascha dodged them all, through luck or chance or wriggling skill.

Until …

Hex's last mud-clod wasn't a mud-clod, it was a stone. Fist-sized, flinty-blue.

His jeans dribbled icy cold water down the backs of

his legs into his socks.

And, without aiming to, without meaning to, the stone struck Sascha on the shoulder.

Sent her spinning.

And she lost her grip and turned upside down before she fell.

Dangled for a while.

Such a slow fall.

The world paused to watch.

So slow.

Hex saw everything.

And he heard the crack of a stick breaking as she landed in the stony stream.

And then the world let out its breath and Sascha let out a cry.

And Hex turned to clay.

He looked up and saw Tommo clinging to the oak tree's trunk, suddenly and seriously sick and pale and staring.

He looked down and saw Sascha lying on her back in the stream, wailing.

Her face was red and wet, and her chest was heaving sobs between the wails, and her right arm was … the wrong shape.

It had a second elbow.

And the stream was bleeding, a thin tentacle of red coiling

away from her, tangling among the stones.

He looked up again and Tommo had vanished.

It was just him and the girl and the water and the woods.

And he couldn't move.

His feet wouldn't lift and he didn't know where they'd take him if they did.

Was he going to run away, leave the scene, deny all knowledge, or was he going to run over and help?

And if he were to help, what would he do? He didn't know what you did for crying kids with weird-shaped arms.

He couldn't move and he couldn't speak. His whole body had hollowed out to a hole. He'd turned from clay to glass. Had become transparent and fragile. One move and he'd shatter into pieces.

And then, before the spell broke, the biggest dog he'd ever seen came padding on huge grey feet out of the shadows towards him.

*Splash, splash*, went its feet along the red-running stream-bed, its nose low, its tongue lolling, its eyes gleaming black.

'Leafy,' called a voice, a woman's voice. 'Leafy! Where've you got to?'

And approaching him was a small bright jolly-looking woman, not *old* old, but older than his mum and dad, a tall walking stick in one hand.

'What've you found there?' she said.

The dog, Leafy, sniffed around the sobbing Sascha and looked

back at its owner, saying nothing.

'Oh my,' said the woman, seeing the girl.

She made her way over, slowly half-scrambling down the shallow bank, leaning on the stick as she went.

'Um,' said Hex, standing there, unmoving.

The dog was almost as tall as he was. It came up to his shoulder, at least. Grey and fuzzy and dim and wiry. Wet eyes sparkling black like stars.

'What's happened?' the woman said, as her great dog *snurfed* at Sascha's face.

Hex didn't know if she was talking to him or to the girl or to the dog.

'Um,' he said again.

Sascha was crying and giggling as the dog stuck its nose in her ear.

The forest looked at him and said nothing.

The woman looked at him and said, 'What did you do?'

*Stupid girl*, Hex thought, suddenly, angrily. *Why'd she have to let go? It's all her fault. Stupid, stupid little girl.*

But he said, 'She fell off the rope-swing.'

'And broke her arm, by the looks,' the woman said.

'Um,' he said, taking a step backwards.

The woman knelt down and touched Sascha's forehead, lifted her up by the shoulders so she was almost sitting, murmured something to her.

'What?' she said, in answer to something Sascha murmured back.

Hex's hollow insides had filled with sick.

If he moved he would spill.

'Who are you?' the woman asked him severely, jolliness having left her.

The dog sat beside her, a hairy grey boulder staring at him with glistening black eyes.

*She's seen you,* he thought. *You can't just say nothing. You can't just leave. Run off. Not like Tommo did. You're in this. Stuck in the middle. You're in trouble, now. All the trouble.*

So he found himself telling a lie.

'She's my little sister,' he said. 'We were mucking about and she slipped … and … fell.'

He looked at what he'd just said.

Why *that* lie?

The woman looked at him, looked him up and down.

'You need to go get help,' she said, after having said nothing. 'Don't you?'

And it was like he'd been waiting for permission.

And he was off, running.

He didn't get far before he hit a problem.

Ahead of him, up the path through the woods, were people,

coming his way, hurrying.

It was Tommo and a grown-up man and a teenager, and there was a buzz about them. Worry. Static in the air.

He dived into a patch of ferns and scrabbled behind a tree, hoping they'd not seen him.

He knew, in his stomach, who they were.

It was Sascha's dad and her older sister, led by Tommo.

Tommo had *gone for help*.

He was a *hero* and Hex was in *hiding*.

He watched as they went by. They didn't see him.

He felt empty and full at the same time.

He waited a little longer. A minute. Two. And then he crept out, back to the path.

He was free to go now, Sascha was safe, he didn't need to call an ambulance or anything, but …

His bike was back by the big oak.

He'd forgotten it when he ran.

It would be a long walk home without it, and what would he say to his dad?

And so …

He followed the path back, through the woods, taking the fork that led up to the top of the high bank. And from up there he saw Sascha's dad kneeling beside her. She was out of the stream now, propped up on the opposite bank.

Her sister, some years older than Hex, was looking pale and

itchy, pulling at her sleeves.

Tommo was sheepish at the back.

The woman and her dog, Leafy, weren't there.

<br>

Tommo and Hex.

They'd been a pair since the day dot.

The two of them against the world, they said.

Dynamic duo.

Everyone knew it.

Born in the same hospital within days of one another.

When their parents had brought them home they'd all kept in touch.

Babysitting duties had been shared, when needed, and the boys had a combined birthday party almost every year.

When they'd gone to school, people had thought they might start to split up, go off and find other friends, that the friendship would dissolve, the way friendships do, naturally and painlessly and with time, but it hadn't.

Even when Tommo's mum had left and his dad had grown cold they kept on, just with Tommo coming round for tea more often than Hex went to his.

After ten years or so they were still best mates.

Hex and Tommo. Tommo and Hex.

Although neither of them would have said it, they loved one another, like brothers.

Hex could've picked his bike up and gone.

Tommo wouldn't dob him in, he knew that.

He could just vanish and no one would ever know. He'd never be blamed.

And, besides, the girl was all right now, wasn't she?

The paramedics arrived, green uniforms glowing, and it was all hushed voices and jolly smiles. They were led by a boy he recognised, Sascha's brother ... Was it Jason? Jackson? Something like that. He was their age, but in the other class at school.

She'd get a lollipop and a sling and all would be well in the world.

Hex was free.

Off the hook.

Out of trouble.

And with that the tension broke and he gave a relieved laugh ...

... which came out louder than was sensible.

('*Why can't you just be sensible, Hector?*')

Everyone down by the brook looked up.

And there he was, a boy by the tree, looking down at them all and laughing. Loudly.

Sascha's big sister said something, pointed, grunted, snarled.

And she was off like a rabbit, like a ferret, like a snake splashing through the water and swerving her way up the root-ladder, even as her dad shouted to stop.

The last thing Hex saw was the look on Tommo's face: guilt, panic, fear, relief, fear, panic, guilt and *embarrassment*.

Hex lifted his bike and ran, again.

When he got home he was clammy and out of breath.

His dad touched his forehead with the back of his fingers as he came in the back door.

'You all right, old boy?' he asked. 'You're all hot and sweaty.'

'Just the cycling,' Hex said. 'You know, up the hill.'

'Ah! Good for the lungs! Fresh air and exercise,' said his dad, turning back to the hob. 'Now, go and wash your hands, lunch is almost ready.'

And then lunch *was* ready and, as it was just the two of them, they sat outside, on the doorstep, eating their fajitas.

Hex couldn't finish his.

'Dad?' he said.

'Yeah?'

He wanted to say something about this morning, but didn't know what.

'When's Frank coming back?'

'Next weekend,' his dad said. 'It's on the calendar.'

Frank was Hex's big sister. She was away on a school trip in France for the holidays.

Normally he didn't want to see her. She was an annoying teenager, playing her music too loud and burying her head in her school books, but right now his heart called for her.

Tommo had *abandoned* him in the woods. Laughed at him. Run off when they should've stuck together.

Hex would've stayed, if Tommo had been the one who'd thrown the stone. Of course he would've. That was what friends did. They stuck together.

And that's what they'd done for years. Forever.

Even when Hex did something that made Tommo groan in class (put both legs in one leg of his shorts when changing for PE, for example, and topple over into the reading corner beanbags), they'd be laughing about it five minutes later.

But … once or twice, in class this last half-term, he'd noticed Tommo *shush* him and get on with his work instead of laughing. Arm down, head down, pen scratching.

Hex had a flash of Tommo's face as Sascha fell.

It was afraid, like a stranger's face.

He'd carried that face in him all the way back from the woods.

'*I'm not angry with you, I'm just disappointed,*' was what Tommo's face said, like a teacher's.

He was worried he'd burnt a bridge too far. That, without meaning to, he'd somehow gone too far, been too ... what? Thoughtless? After all those years, could Sascha's arm be the straw that broke their friendship's back?

He couldn't have *said* any of this to his sister, just as he couldn't say any of it to his dad, or to Tommo, just as he couldn't really say any of it to himself, not in *words*, just as a faint sick feeling swirling in his stomach.

But ...

But Frank would've smiled at him, as she sometimes did, and rub her knuckle on the top of his head and call him a dummy and tell him to get out of her room and the world would be *normal* again, not perfect, not sorted, but *normal*. It would be like it was before the stone had flown.

Normal.

But instead it was just him and his dad and his thoughts and the memory of the morning.

'You not gonna eat that, old chap?' his dad said, pointing at the wrap in Hex's hand.

'Not hungry.'

'You do look pale,' his dad said, looking at him. He softly touched Hex's forehead again. 'Perhaps, you should have a lie-down. I think you've maybe caught the sun a bit.'

And so that's what Hex did, while his dad finished his unfinished fajita.

Hex slept all afternoon and woke up just in time for tea.

He didn't dream.

And he didn't feel any better as he sat at the dining table.

His mum was home from work and as she pushed at the salad with her fork said, 'You look good, Hector dear, did you have a nice day?'

And he was halfway through thinking about what he could say when her mobile buzzed on the table and she looked down at the message that had just arrived and it was something she had to answer right away, to do with work, and he was let off the hook.

# MONDAY NIGHT

As Hex tried to sleep, for the second time that day, he found one sound repeating in his ears, above the murmur of the talking book playing in the dark room.

Sascha's arm.

*The cracking of a stick over your knee.*

Sascha's arm.

*The crack of a stick under foot.*

Sascha's arm.

A *crack in the shadows.*

Worry swam inside him.

Worry about what his dad would say when Sascha's dad phoned up or came round, as he was bound to.

Even if Tommo hadn't dobbed him in, given them his name, then Sascha's brother knew who he was. Everyone knew Hex (knew *of* Hex, he corrected himself … no one *knew* Hex), even if they'd never spoken. He was noticeable, he knew that.

But it hadn't been his fault.

Deep water swirled in his stomach.

It was Sascha who'd followed *them.*

It was Sascha who'd *insisted* on going on the swing.

It was Sascha who'd *let go* of the rope.

They had no right to blame *him* for any of this.

And so the worry-tumble went on, until he fell asleep and woke up again.

# TUESDAY

After breakfast Hex got on his bike and cycled over to Tommo's house.

The sunshine had washed away the shadows of the night, of the day before.

He thought this would be a new day of mucking about on their bikes, scuffing up and down the kerbs and maybe swinging high on the proper swings down the rec. Renewed and reset. Just another school holiday day.

But Tommo said he couldn't come out. Had to help his dad with something or other.

He sort of looked over Hex's shoulder as he said it.

Hex let out a dwindling, stuttering laugh and followed up with a string of loud armpit farts, but even that didn't make Tommo look at him properly. That'd always made him fall about before. It was guaranteed gold.

Tommo shook his head vaguely and said, 'Hex,' in an almost-sad sigh.

'Well, OK,' Hex said, picking his bike up and cycling away. 'Later.'

A knot inside him twisted as he cycled, caught in the turning wheels, pulled him down deeper into his head.

Although the sun was hot and the air bright, a shadow sat on his shoulder.

One stupid girl breaking her arm (little kids broke things all the time, their bones were softer, easy to mend) had broken something between Tommo and him.

Years of friendship, snapped in two.

It was daft.

So stupid.

And, he thought, if Tommo had let it come between them, if he was too cowardly to hold a hand out over that gap, down from the top of the riverbank, and pull Hex up from the cold stream, to say, 'It doesn't matter, it wasn't your fault, buddy,' then … well, then

Hex was probably better off without him.

And that was that.

Except it wasn't.

He could see Tommo's face, pale and looking up at him from beside the broken girl, and something was falling away from him, something he couldn't name.

The raw screaming blare of a car's horn, and the whoosh of hot metal passing close by, brought him shockingly, suddenly back to himself.

He rested a foot on the kerb as he shuddered to a stop.

The sun was high and the shadows were short beneath him.

There were other doors he could go and knock on (doors of kids who'd say, 'Oh. Hey. Hector? What're you doing here … ?'), other kids he could bump into out in the street and tag along with ('Yeah, s'pose, if you wanna …'), but none of them were Tommo.

The dynamic duo.

Practically brothers.

And so Hex circled the streets on his bike alone, kicking dust in the gutters, bouncing off the kerbs, zooming along the straights, feet blurring on the pedals. Letting the air into his head.

There was only so much of this he could handle though, and

soon Hex made his mind up to just go home.

But his dad didn't believe in kids being indoors when the sun was shining. It was to do with having grown up in the rain or something, and so he'd probably end up having to do weeding in the garden rather than being allowed to lie on his bed and read his comics, but, he thought, even that would be better than being alone out here on his bike.

And so Hex was surprised when he found himself freewheeling down the hill past the level crossing, heading back towards the woods.

Instead of turning off into the close, where Sascha might be sitting in her front garden, with her broken arm, he kept on the main road and found himself cycling slowly along the edge of the woods.

It looked a lot less *foresty* from here, with the road behind him and a pavement and a low wooden fence between him and the trees.

He hoicked his bike up the kerb and walked it along to the path that led into the side of the forest. There was another red dog-mess bin and another sign from the council saying how much they cared about keeping *some* nature around.

He walked into the shadows.

Immediately, cooler.

Ah.

Immediately, better.

*Oh.*

Being here was good.

The trees were filled with life-going-on.

Birds sang, squirrels leapt, leaves glowed and it all spoke to him, saying nothing.

Nothing at all.

He wasn't thinking any more, which was good.

Thinking got you into trouble.

One thought led to another, and when the first thought was a bad thought, the next one would look at it and shrink away, or ruck its shoulders and try to be even worse.

Thoughts fought one another and the biggest and hardest ones won, and they weren't always kind. (And you couldn't even distract them with a joke, not like other kids.)

There was that time he didn't think, just before half-term, when Alfie Eaves had wet himself in class. The smell caught everyone's attention.

Miss Short had found him some fresh trousers from the lost property box, but Hex had got hold of the wet ones at break and had danced with them across the playground, holding them between his fingertips, and singing a song he'd just made up.

Everyone had laughed and laughed (wet themselves laughing,

you might've said), all except Alfie, and Miss Short, when she saw.

He hadn't *thought* about it, one thing had simply followed another, and the song and dance had just happened as he'd watched, with everyone else, and he'd liked the laughter, but afterwards …

After he'd been in the head's office, again …

And after he'd got home with the letter for his mum and dad …

And after he'd gone to bed … the thoughts had come.

*Why?*

*Why do this?*

*Why do this to that boy?*

*Why do this to yourself?*

And the thoughts had shown him Alfie's face when he'd seen Hex dancing. It had been more embarrassed, more crumpled up, than the face he'd worn when Miss Short had led him out of the classroom, dripping.

*Too much squash at break. Accidents happen.*

But it was his own fault, the stupid kid, peeing in class. Who does that?

*Baby.*

And it was just a joke, a bit of fun. Why'd he have to get so wound up when he saw Hex with his trousers?

*Stupid kid.*

And that should have been the end of the thoughts, that

last *stupid kid*, but it wasn't.

It never was.

Lying in bed he'd felt like two people: one who did stuff and one who watched, and neither of them understood the other.

And in his memory he'd seen Tommo laughing along. *Everyone* had laughed. But the following morning, as they'd walked to school, he'd not said anything about it, in such a way that Hex heard.

And Hex recognised the silence, because it was the same way something inside him had said nothing.

But here … here, under the trees, in the green shade, with life all around, on his own but no longer lonely, wheeling his bike down the dirt path on that sunny morning, birdsong in his ears, Hex didn't think about Alfie or about Sascha or about Tommo or about any of it …

His mind was an open blank.

Free.

Clear.

Clean.

And for a few seconds, happiness looked in, smiling.

Hex found himself back at the rope-swing's oak, standing on the high bank, the stream below him, spotted with the pale domes of dry stones.

Again he heard the crack of a branch underfoot.

*Stupid girl. What had she been thinking, letting go?*

And then he heard it again.

Behind him.

And he turned and there they were, Sascha's brother and sister, crashing through the green towards him.

One of them yanked Hex's bike from his hands, threw it to one side.

'What the hell were you playing at?' the sister said, poking him in the chest, her finger a spear.

'It was her,' he said. '*She* followed *us*. It weren't our idea.'

'You know she had to go to *hospital?*' the sister jabbed. 'They said she might *never draw again*, fracture's that bad. And she *loves* drawing.'

The brother bobbed in the background, peering round the teenage girl, glaring at Hex, but saying nothing.

'We d-d-didn't do nothing,' Hex stuttered. 'She f-f-followed us and wouldn't stop. Bouncing about. She … she … she wouldn't *stop* …'

And then Sascha's sister punched him.

⸮

Hex's head cracked back and he staggered, the world spinning, his teeth buzzing.

'That's for Sascha,' the brother shouted.

'You don't let someone do that to your family,' the sister hissed, 'not to a little kid like that, who can't even fight back. You're the worst sort of bully.'

She planted her hand square on his chest and pushed.

Hex staggered and fell to the ground … but the ground wasn't there and he tumbled through empty air, banged roots on the way down the high bank, and rolled, rolled, rolled, bruised, burst and bloodied, right up to the edge of the stream.

The crossbar of the rope-swing was motionless above him.

He scrambled to his feet, swearing with the best, harshest words he knew, touched his fiery lip and saw his hand come away wet and red.

His mouth tasted of metal.

Then he heard movement above and they were coming for him, unsatisfied with what they'd done, descending the high bank, scuffling in the dirt, splashing through the water, slipping on stepping stones, and he clambered up the opposite bank and hared off up into the ferns.

His head spun.

His stomach froze.

His feet squelched.

He ran like his life depended on it.

He'd never been punched before, not that he could remember.

There was a physical pain in that punch, of course, that throbbed in his lip, in his teeth, across his face, but it had gone through the flesh into his spirit too, bruising with humiliation and shock.

And there is no plaster for that, no salve or bandage or cold compress that can soothe a stunned ego.

Ferns slapped at his legs as he ran through a sea of them, trees flicking by on either side.

The crash of his feet filled his ears, along with his thudding heart. There was shouting somewhere behind him.

And as he ran, as he fell forwards into the forest, he was aware of a shadow moving through the trees off to one side.

He slammed into a thick trunk, clasped it with his hands, pulled himself round it, and pushed off the other side, and that shadow, of something grey and huge and dark, flickered between the trees to his left.

And then he was out of the ferns, pushing through tangles of sticky bindweed and goosegrass and nettles and scrub, ducking beneath low branches, off the path entirely, off the map.

And the shadow kept pace.

And it was a wolf.

There in the forest, the darkest of greys, a loop of shadow, loping in and out of the light on great silent feet.

A wolf, pacing beside him.

Sascha's siblings somewhere behind him and a great wolf beside him.

He was done for.

Caught between the headlights and the hard place.

*You can't escape this*, he thought.

And suddenly the clinging weeds let up and as he staggered forward, a stitch in his side, the last breaths burning in his throat, a fatal wobble taking charge of his legs, he found the trees giving way, and the ground beneath his feet was suddenly grassy, flat, free of the woods' tripping roots.

*

He was in a clearing, like you read about in books.

A proper fairy-tale clearing.

Across from him the forest started up again, dark, forbidding, ancient, curling, massive, but here, in a circle, there was nothing but an open sky, grey and stormy-looking, above.

And there was a cottage.

That was the only word for it.

A cottage.

One storey, with a thatched roof and those windows that were small already but seemed even smaller by being made of dozens of little diamonds of glass held together by criss-crossed metal bands.

Smoke coiled from the chimney.

A woodshed leant against one wall, and a well, with one of those little roofs of its own and a bucket on a rope with a handle and winch, stood off a little way to one side.

And, as Hex looked, heaving breaths, and clutching his chest, out of the forest to his left paced the great wolf, as high as his shoulder and as dark as dreamless sleep, and he could've wept with fear, *would've* wept with fear, had his face not already been wet with shock and pain, anger and blood.

He staggered backwards, like he'd been punched, again.

But then he saw that it *wasn't* a wolf, but a dog.

And he remembered that he'd forgotten the dog he'd seen in the woods the day before.

And this was *that* dog.

And it looked at him with great sad black eyes.

His mind whirred like a hard drive waking up, and gave him the dog's name.

'Leafy,' he said.

The dog said nothing back.

Hex walked towards the cottage with Leafy by his side.

His face ached.

His ribs ached.

His feet ached.

His lungs ached.

His eyes ached.

His teeth ached.

His heart ached.

His bruises ached, and they were most of him just now.

Leafy leant close to him and he put an arm across the dog's back.

The dog was firm, solid, warm.

This wasn't a dream.

He hadn't hit his head on the way down the riverbank and started hallucinating.

This was real, and yet …

The door to the cottage opened and a woman came out, the same woman he'd seen with Leafy the day before, stick in hand, and as she did so the clouds gave a grumble and fat spots of rain started to fall.

'Bring him in,' she said.

And Hex didn't know if she was saying it to him, or to the dog.

Hex collapsed into a huge soft armchair.

There was smoke in the air.

An unsteady light from an open fire.

The smell of wood, and of fresh baking. Fresh bread.

Heat. Hot. Crackle.

'What happened to you?' the woman asked, kneeling, with some effort, beside him.

Hex didn't answer.

He didn't know how to answer.

What should he say?

The dog padded around the room. A rumbling shadow, like the underside of a table, stalking on lanky tall legs.

Silence stretched.

The woman dabbed at his split lip with a damp flannel.

'Looks like you've been in a scrap,' she said.

Dab. Dab. Dab.

'We met,' he muttered. 'Before.'

'Did we?' she said, looking into his face.

'Yesterday,' he said.

Part of him didn't want to remind her.

Part of him knew she already knew.

She dabbed the blood away in silence for a moment before saying, 'Oh, that poor girl. Yes, you *were* there, weren't you?'

'Yes,' he said.

She dabbed a little more, then went over to a dresser, chose a small pot from among many and brought it back over to him.

'This will sting,' she said.

Her hands were soft and wrinkled and her nails were unpainted. She smelt of apples, or pears, or some other fruit.

With the corner of a clean cloth she smeared a little ointment from the pot on to his swollen lip, and on to a cut he didn't know he had above his ear, and then on to his scratched hands.

And she was right, it did sting, and his eyes watered, but he didn't move.

The dog, Leafy, padded around them, and then slumped to the floor and rested its head on his knees. Shadows swirled against the walls in the corner of his eye. The firelight flickered, and then they settled.

'She likes you,' the woman said. 'She's called Leafy.'

'I know,' said Hex. 'I heard you say it yesterday.'

Hex rubbed his hands together, smearing and smoothing the ointment out across all the scratches and rubbing it on his scraped knee.

'She's Leafy and I'm Missus,' she said, as she returned the pot to the shelf. 'You can call me that. We don't much stand on ceremony these days.'

She poked the fire with a metal stick and then placed a fresh log on, poked again, let the flames find their way round the new wood.

'What's your name?' she asked, turning back to him. 'What's your story?'

She lowered herself into an armchair on the other side of the fire.

Her eyes sparkled as the rain pattered at the door and windows.

He didn't want to answer. His mind kept drifting back to the fight, back to how it hadn't been a fight at all, back to how he hadn't even had a chance to hit back, to defend himself. They'd taken him by surprise. It had been – it *was* – uneven, unbalanced, unfair.

He was bubbling, antsy, angry and embarrassed (and angry that he was embarrassed, and vice versa, spiralling down).

'I'm Hex,' he said, when the silence had stretched out too far.

'That's an unusual name,' Missus said. 'It sounds, if I may say, ill-fated, ill-starred. I'd look for another one. You know, to be on the safe side.'

She was so calm, the way she said it, so friendly, even though the words sounded almost scolding, unfriendly.

It was confusing and it didn't soothe his anger.

'Oh,' he said. 'It's short. I mean it's short for … for Hector.'

He could feel his swollen lip stretch each time he spoke, tight and fat and hot. The pain was distant though, a good sort of pain, like poking a bruise. Half numb, half alive.

'Oh,' the woman said. 'Now *there's* a name.'

'It's stupid,' Hex said.

He'd been half-teased for that name for as long as he remembered. A daft name that didn't quite fit, like hand-me-down socks from some long-dead uncle with huge feet. He didn't fit it, he didn't *feel* it. He half-hated it.

'Stupid?' she said, leaning back in her chair.

'Posh,' he said, snapping at her. 'Just stupid.'

She laughed.

'Posh? Oh! Yes! He *was* a prince, after all. The noblest man to walk the fields of Ilium. Brave beyond reason, yet loath to fight. A man among men. Sad Priam's son. A charming smile, but always a cloud crossing his face.'

And then she spoke in a foreign language, words that had the rhythm of poetry, like dark waves on the sand, and when she stopped speaking she smiled sadly at the shadows that had crept down the walls and out from under the chairs to listen, and then looked at him and said, '*You* have been wounded in battle too. No, my little modern Hector?'

And only now did he really wonder at the oddness of *everything*. *Only now?*

This woman who spoke so strangely.

This cottage in a clearing that couldn't possibly fit in the woods he knew.

The rain that was drumming on the windows from heavy dark clouds that hadn't been there twenty minutes earlier.

Oddness held the door open for fear to step in.

'I think I'd best get going,' he said.

Leafy huffed on his lap, a deep dog-sigh.

'Have something hot to drink first,' the woman said. 'Wait for the rain to let up. You'll catch your death if you go out in that. And besides …'

She heaved herself out of her chair and put a kettle on the stovetop.

Hex leant back, looked around.

The cottage was cosy, lit and warmed by the fireplace.

The ceiling above him was whitewashed, but it was shadowy, smoked by years of the open fire, and only softly reached by the firelight.

Between two thick black beams, over near the door, he noticed a bundle hanging, strapped to the plaster ceiling, like she'd netted useless old unneeded things there, not having an attic to shove them in. He thought of those filmy bundles of spider-eggs you sometimes found in the corner of a window.

From the kitchen-end of the room Missus said, as she rattled some cups out of a cupboard, 'Hector, dear. I've got a proposition for you. An offer, you might say.'

Hector wanted to get up and go, but Leafy was half-snoring in his lap and, as she did so, her upper lip curled back and ivory-yellow teeth glistened in black gums and he didn't dare move.

There was darkness inside her mouth, between those teeth.

The kettle whistled and as Missus poured steaming water into the cups she said, 'It pains me to see a fellow brought low like this. One so young, given such an unfair drubbing.'

She handed him one of the cups.

'How many were there?'

He let the heat scorch his palms and his fingers.

'Two,' he said.

'Yes. And look, you are just one.'

She shook her head, tutting.

'And the girl is older. By some years, yes?' she said. 'So unfair.'

He nodded.

She took a big slurp of tea.

'Don't you wish you could do something?'

He said nothing.

'Get your own back, I mean,' she said. 'Hector? The unfairness of it, the injustice, bubbles out of you.'

Hex said nothing.

'I can help,' she said.

'I can even the score,' she said.

'I can make it so they never hurt you again,' she said.

And as she spoke she leant forward and smiled, firelight flickering across her cheeks, stars in the depths of her dark eyes.

And Leafy lifted her head from his lap and turned round three times before lying down in front of the flames.

⚬

'All you have to do is ask,' Missus said, after the dog had settled.

'Ask what?' he asked.

'Ask us for revenge, Hector,' she said softly. 'And we shall see to it.'

The walls of the cottage grew closer, saying nothing.

The only light seemed to come from the woman herself. It was just them and the shadows.

'You've been *hurt*. Fallen and bruised and *humiliated* in battle. But you have the chance to right that wrong, Hector. One word from you and we shall clip them from the world. That is Leafy's gift. *Our* gift to you. A simple thing.'

He wanted to move, to get up and walk out, but something held him in place.

It *had* been unfair. She was right about that. They'd turned on him for something he *hadn't even done*.

The hot tea in his hands was undrunk.

He was more afraid than he'd ever been. Deeply, silently afraid. This was all real.

He was falling and falling and falling, and it wouldn't stop.

Rain lashed the windows.

Shadows slid across the ceiling, peering down at him.

'And what will you do?' he said. 'I mean … to *them*?'

'We will simply persuade the world to forget them.'

She snapped her fingers.

Leafy looked up, panted in the fireplace's red glow.

'Like that,' she said. 'Leafy will bite and they shall be gone, as if they'd never been. Only *you* would know they'd ever existed at all. And your world will heal, reshape itself around the hole. It's more elastic than you might suppose. No one will miss them or remember them. No one will be hurt by their loss, not mother nor father nor loyal pet. We would not inflict that cruelness on anyone, we just wish to help *you*.'

'That sounds, um …' Hex began, 'a bit … uh, much? *Excessive?* Is that the word?'

Missus smiled and her moist teeth twinkled in the firelight.

'That's the right word,' she nodded. 'The one you want. But it's not *true*.' Her eyes darkened, and she leant closer. The fire popped and crackled and dimmed in the hearth. '*Excessive* would be to leave revenge to the humans. That way it never ends. The tit for tat, the back and forth, the endless feud. An eye for an eye, and a tooth for a tooth, and a child for a child, leaves the world eyeless, toothless and childless. "You killed my sister, so I killed your brother, so you killed my son, so I killed your cousin …" I've sat helpless across ages watching, the world beyond our reach spiralling in sorrow. We are just one woman and her dog … But where we *can* … where we're *asked* … Leafy and I make a single snip, one small *excision*, and the cycle of revenge stops turning at the first turn. We help the world. We *save* it.'

She suddenly looked away from Hex and turned to the fire.

'Will it hurt?' he asked.

'Them?'

'Yes.'

'No.' She chuckled. 'We are not monsters, Hector. They will know nothing. Their loved ones will know nothing. No one will be hurt, and *you* will feel *better* knowing you've taken some nastiness out of the world.'

The rain spattered against the window in a sudden squall.

The chimney moaned softly and the fire glowed with a flurry of red sparks.

'OK,' he said.

'OK?' she said.

The grass glinted like jewellery.

In his pocket was an acorn Missus had given him.

'Sleep on it,' she had said. 'And if you are certain, crush this and we shall come in the night and smooth the world out while you sleep. If not, leave it, forget us, and the world will remain the same. Our gift is not to be taken lightly. Never let it be said we *encouraged* you, or *rushed* you, or *forced* you. No, no.'

Hex wanted to get home and see his dad and his mum.

The woods were dark and smelt of rain.

He kept one hand on Leafy's shoulder as she led the way.

After a few minutes of up and down and under and over he recognised where he was, back in the woods he knew.

'I'm home,' he said, and in a way he was.

Leafy gave a *snurf*, and turned and brushed past him, walking back the way they'd come, tail swishing gently as she went.

Hex turned to watch her and found the almost invisible hum of the electric fence at the edge of the woods straight before him, and he was looking out at the farmer's fields (green stalks swayed) and he saw just a shadow fading in the stunning sunlight, greyness eaten away by dazzle.

The sky was blue. There had been no rain.

He looked at his watch for the first time in what felt like hours and found that it had been. It was almost lunchtime. His dad would've started cooking already.

He hurried through the woods, his aches present but numbed, his swollen lip tight, fat and dominating.

When he reached the stream he stopped.

There was his bike, at the foot of the high bank, wheels buckled, chain off, brake cables pulled from their sockets.

It had been stomped.

*The anger didn't go away.*

He lifted it up.

*The unfairness didn't stop.*

The wheels dragged, instead of turning.

It took forever to get it home.

Every passing car stared at him.

Every person out walking a dog or pushing a pushchair stared.

Every cat lounging in a front garden or a front window watched him pass by, slowly, trudging up the hill.

The boy with the bruises, with the split lip, with the scrap metal on his shoulder.

He'd wanted to give up.

He hated this being *seen*, being *noticed*.

The sun shone down, punishing him.

The pavement stared up, the tarmac sticky, and smelling like it had been freshly laid.

The world was laughing.

(There is an age-old difference between 'with' and 'at'. 'Laughing *with* you' means you were in control (such as when you danced for joy in the playground), 'laughing *at* you' means you weren't (such as when someone else was dancing with your wet trousers, singing your name). Today he knew which side of that dance he was on, and the world found it hilarious.)

He was weeping by the time he pushed open the back gate, with frustration and anger and tension and embarrassment and the sheer physical effort of carry-dragging that bike uphill for so long.

He dumped it on the patio and sat down on the back step, shuddering.

There were too many thoughts stuck circling in his brain. Vultures waiting for him to give up.

❧

His dad found him there a few minutes later.

'Heck,' he said, a jolly tone in his voice. '*There* you are. Just in time. I've made corn-on-the-cob *and* salad *and* chicken skewers. Shall we eat out here again? It's another beautiful d—'

And then he stopped, because he saw the state of things.

'Good God,' he said, rushing over and kneeling down. 'What happened to you? Are you OK?'

He lifted Hex's chin, gently, with one hand, and looked from the boy to the bike to the boy again.

'Did you get knocked down?' he asked. 'By a car? Or … ?'

Hex shook his head.

His dad was a blur.

And then he was being hugged, tight and warm, and he could smell hot spices and cool cotton.

And then he said, 'Ow, not so tight.'

And he sniffed a dribble of snot right up his nose, so hard it bounced off his brain and made him sneeze, all down the back of his dad's shirt.

And his dad laughed.

And he laughed.

And for a moment all was well in the world.

His dad made him go upstairs to get changed, and he followed with the first-aid kit.

'I'm glad you're OK,' he said, as he put plasters where plasters went.

Hex sniffed, sitting there, on his bed in his pants.

'It wasn't a car?' his dad asked.

'No,' said Hex.

His dad breathed a sigh of relief.

'Then,' his dad went on, rummaging in Hex's drawers for some clean clothes, 'I shall ask no more. I was a boy once, I know what it's like. It's tough growing up. Finding your place, finding where

you fit. You're always gonna get into a scrap or two, loose a few punches, lose a few fights. And it's none of my business, not unless you *want* to tell me, in which case …'

Hex was filled with love at that moment, but also the dread fear that his dad was going to begin one of the 'stories of his youth'. It was something he and Frank agreed on: when their dad declared, '*When I was a boy …*' their eyes would meet across the dining table and Frank would do a most monumental eye-roll and they'd both laugh.

But his dad didn't go off on one. Instead he said, 'You don't have to tell me, Heck, but we're gonna have to tell your mum something. We can fix the bike, but we can't hide that fat lip or that shiner.'

'The rope-swing,' Hex said after a moment. 'I fell off the rope-swing.'

His dad nodded.

'Yes. Good thinking. We'll tell her that. Good story!'

'It's true,' said Hex. 'It's what happened.'

He pulled a new pair of trousers on, and a fresh T-shirt, and they went and had lunch.

Hex's dad needed to go to the library that afternoon. He had some books to take back and wanted to get some new ones out.

He had lessons to prepare, school started back next week and he'd been tasked with covering 'The Causes of the First World War' while Mr Kydd was off on paternity leave.

'I did it at school,' he said, 'but that was a million years ago. It was all in one ear and out the other. Something about a great duck getting shot or something.'

Hex pretended to listen, but he was really just watching a bird circling overhead. A black speck high up, wings spread wide, not flapping, not doing anything but circling round and round on the invisible air. So weightless and free, up there, just a shadowed silhouette against the endless blue.

'You can stay here if you like,' his dad was saying, 'or you could come with. It's up to you. You know, if you need a lie-down.'

'I had a lie-down yesterday,' Hex said. 'I'm not a baby, always napping.'

'Didn't say you were, Heck, old chap,' he said, smiling. 'Maybe have a bath to soothe the bruises and get a bit of peace and quiet.'

That didn't sound like a stupid idea, so Hex went and found the books of his that needed returning and put them on the kitchen table. Then he went and put the plug in, poured a big glug of bubble bath and turned the taps on.

Out of the bath, dried off and dressed, but still with damp hair and that warm feeling all over, he sat down in front of the computer.

Logged on.

Put in his postcode, and let the internet load the map.

He dragged the image around and around, and found what he knew he'd find.

Nothing.

No clearing.

No cottage.

Nothing but trees.

And the road on one side.

And the fields on the other.

Just as expected: the woods were just the woods.

In Hex's head it proved two things. Both of which couldn't be true together.

On the one hand, it proved that what had happened this morning, after he'd got beaten up, hadn't *really* happened. He *couldn't't've* run through the woods and found himself in a fairy-tale clearing. He hadn't ended up going into some strange old woman's cottage, because it *wasn't on the map*.

On the other hand, because he *had* gone to the cottage, that meant it had been *somewhere else*, had been some*thing* else … Not finding it on the map just proved that Missus and Leafy were … *magic* or whatever.

He zoomed out.

Just a tapering finger of woodland pointing away from town, dwindling into the thin dark line of the brook running under a bridge and off the top of the screen.

Then there was a ring at the doorbell.

Then a knock.

Twice.

Three times.

Hex opened the door, even as the silence in his head told him not to.

He should wait for his dad to come home. Should pretend to be out.

Today had been enough already.

On the doorstep stood a woman he didn't know, beside a child he did.

It was Sascha and her – he assumed – mother.

'Is this him?' the woman said.

'Look, I got a slung,' Sascha said to Hex cheerily. 'And I got to pick the colour.'

'It's "*sling*",' said a voice from behind the pair.

Sascha's sister was lurking back there, digging dirt out from between paving slabs with her toe.

'Is this him?' repeated the mother.

'Look,' said Sascha, holding her plaster-covered arm up out of its sling for Hex to see.

'It's white,' he said, finding his words at last.

'Yep,' said Sascha proudly. 'It's *classic*. Helga Ironside got a pink one when she fell off the horses, and Tony Thingie had a green one, but that's just showing off if you ask me.'

Her mother gave an almost-laugh and asked, for a third time, 'Are you the boy who did this?'

Hex stammered without saying anything.

His lip started throbbing.

'It … it was an ac— an accident,' he said, pushing the words out through a throat that wanted nothing to do with them.

'An *accident?*' the mother said sharply. 'That's not what I heard. I heard you knocked her off … And what was she doing with you in the first place? What were you doing with her? Look at me when I talk to you.'

'Swings,' said Sascha, beaming.

She was rummaging in the pockets of her dungarees with her good hand.

'She … she followed us,' Hex said weakly.

He could feel himself shaking. Growing paler by the second.

'Is there an adult home?' asked the mother, looking over his head. 'Someone in charge of you?'

Just as she said that, Hex heard the back door slam.

The sun was hot.

'My dad,' whispered Hex.

'Good,' the woman said. 'I want him to see what you did to my little darling. Poor Sascha. The doctors said she'll be lucky if the arm sets straight. It's her favourite arm.'

'Sign it?' said Sascha, waving a marker pen.

There was a sigh from her sister, still hanging back, pacing tigerishly behind them.

'Hex?' called his dad from the kitchen.

Hex took the pen but didn't say anything.

He had the feeling that this meeting wasn't going the way

anyone had planned it, except perhaps Sascha.

Footsteps behind him in the hall.

'Oh, there you are. Who's that?'

'Are you this boy's father?' said Sascha's mum sharply.

'Yes,' said Hex's dad, resting a hand on Hex's shoulder. 'Larry Patel. And you are … ?'

'I hope you've punished him properly.'

'Punished? Sorry?'

She pointed at Sascha, who was still holding her plastered arm up.

Hex still hadn't taken the lid off the pen.

'He broke my daughter's arm. Didn't he mention it?'

Hex's dad was quiet.

Hex shrank.

It had been *her* fault, the stupid girl following them, and not hanging on properly, but now everyone was looking at *him*.

Sascha bobbed urgently, waving her arm.

Her sister stood still.

'He didn't think to mention it?'

'Um, no. Not *exactly*.'

There was a pause.

'Hector? Is there something you want to tell me?'

His hand was still on Hex's shoulder.

'Mmm?' said Sascha's mother.

'It was an accident,' said Hex quietly. 'We were mucking about down the rope-swing … and she … she fell off.'

'Oh, yes. The rope-swing,' his dad said. 'You did mention that. That's where you got those cuts and that fat lip. Look,' he said, crouching to look in his son's face, but talking to the woman. 'There's a nasty black eye coming up there.'

It was as if Sascha's mother looked at Hex properly for the first time.

She leant down, took his chin in her hand and turned his head this way and that, firmly but not painfully.

'I figured,' his dad said, 'he'd got in a bit of a fight this morning, but I didn't know it was with a little girl. Hector?'

'*This morning?* This is *yesterday* we're talking about,' the woman said.

Hex's eyes flickered helplessly towards the sister, and the mother turned.

'Maria,' she snapped. 'What did you do?'

She straightened up.

The sister's cheeks flushed and she muttered something like, 'He got what was coming to him.'

But her mother clearly didn't think much of the words and, leaning straight over Sascha's head, she swung her arm out and slapped the older girl across the cheek.

'No fighting,' she said, pointing her finger like a wand. 'You've been warned before. You don't flipping well hit stupid little kids. First you lose Sascha, then you pick a fight. No! It's not on!'

The sister, Maria, took a step backwards, her hand clapped to her stinging cheek, her tear-glittered eyes glued on Hex's as her mother turned back to the man and the boy in the doorway.

'Sorry about that,' she said, smiling jaggedly. 'Looks like it's apologies all round, eh?'

Hex and his dad both were silent and pale.

Sascha sighed theatrically, shook her head and tugged at Hex's sleeve.

'Come on,' she said. 'Sign it.'

And Hex knelt down and pulled the lid off the pen, and wrote '*I'm really sorry about you're arm*'.

'It really was an accident,' he mumbled. 'A stupid accident. I'm sorry.'

'Maria,' the mother half-hissed. 'What do you say?'

And Maria, out on the pavement, let the limp word 'sorry' fall, wriggling, on to the ground between them.

'Good, good,' said the mother.

'Um, yes,' said Hex's dad.

'Gotta go now,' said Sascha, putting the pen back in a pocket and spinning with her plastered arm in the air like some sort of cyborg ballerina. 'Places to be, people to see.'

Her mum patted her head absently, as if petting a strange creature that had just walked out of the forest, one she didn't understand in the least, but which she had promised the king she'd look after, and they turned to go.

As Hex watched them leave, Maria, the sister, still rubbing

her red cheek, glanced at him and slipped, with her spare hand, something out of her pocket.

It was small and green and roundish, and she dropped it, stepped back and crunched it under her heel, before grinding it with a twist, flashing him one last lightning look, and skulking off after the others.

And then it was over.

It was just Hex and his dad in the doorway, and the door was being shut and the world was being told to stay outside.

'Sit down.'

Hex sat on the stairs.

The sun, which had ignored the injunction to stay outside, lit his dad from behind, making him look like a shadow risen up above him, a shadow with something to say, a shadow that hardly knew where to begin.

'What the hell have you been playing at?'

Hex said nothing.

'This is serious stuff, Heck. A broken arm ... a little girl's broken arm ... *That* can't be ignored ... even an accident. You *should've* told me. You should've told me *straight away*. They shouldn't have to traipse up here to get an apology out of you. That's just not on. We should've been down there first thing, offering our olive branch. Never mind the rest.'

Hex sniffled.

'Look,' his dad said, quieter, stepping forward and sitting beside him on the stairs. 'Budge up. There. Now tell me what happened.'

Hex looked up to see them both reflected in the hallway mirror. They were bright, lit by the sun.

And he began, haltingly, with tears, to tell most of the truth.

'We don't hit back,' his dad said. 'That's the one rule, Heck. You hurt her sister, by accident. But even if you'd done it on purpose, she shouldn't have hit you like that. And you don't hit her back, not ever. This is what civilisation is for, an end to the old eye-for-an-eye business.'

'But how … What about revenge, Dad? You've gotta get your own back – don't you? I mean, if someone hurts you.'

'Or the people you love?'

'Yeah.'

'Well, you can simply choose not to,' his dad said. 'Or you appeal to authority. You're a kid, *my* kid, so it's my place to think up the punishment. In the same way it's that girl's mum's place to think up the punishment for her.'

'She hit her.'

Hex's dad was silent for a moment.

'Yes,' he said. 'Easy answers are rarely the right ones. And a slap like that's so easy. But what will it teach her?' He paused again. 'I think you've had punishment enough, watching that, getting your fat lip … and seeing how happy you made that little girl with her plaster cast.'

He chuckled softly before going quiet again.

'Are you going to tell Mum?' Hex asked.

His dad looked at him in the mirror.

He shook his head.

'Nah, our secret. You fell off the rope-swing, yeah?'

'Yeah,' said Hex.

After his dad had left him, Hex opened the front door.

He went into the front garden and out to the pavement.

The sound of the slap across the girl's – Maria's – face echoed among the birdsong and sunshine, and he thought of the softness of his dad's voice.

How some of us are born to kindness.

Even if it doesn't always feel that way.

He was happy he had his dad and not Maria's mum. The sort of person who would do something like that, something *humiliating* like that, in front of these other people, these strangers …

He shook the thought out of his head before it went any further.

He knelt down and found what he'd feared.

There, on the pavement, where Maria had ground her heel, was a broken acorn. Its little brown cup was cracked into pieces and the bright green skin shone across the fluffy smush of the insides.

He knew what it was.

He knew what had happened.

He hadn't been made the only offer.

He hadn't been the only one who'd found the cottage.

He hadn't been the only one Missus and Leafy had welcomed into their home.

His heart fluttered out of his mouth and flew away.

He slumped, empty, to the tarmac.

He pushed the crushed acorn with his finger and a tiny shadow slithered out and slid away across the road.

Well, he thought, he was still here. Nothing had happened.

He hadn't been cut out of the world.

Hadn't been forgotten.

Not yet.

Of course it was all nonsense, had all been nonsense – a dream his banged head had dreamt up.

But then he also remembered Missus's words: 'Crush this and we shall come in the night.'

And he saw her little white teeth glint moistly in the firelight.

And he feared.

And his fear echoed inside his hollow chest, its drone drowning out his dad's words, his appeal to kindness.

And the need, the necessity, the importance, of getting his own back reared up. (It was only right, anyone would agree.) If she'd done it to him, he had to do it back to her.

The stupid bully-girl was asking for it.

He rushed inside, letting the door slam shut behind him, and ran upstairs.

He'd patted the pockets of the trousers he had on and his acorn hadn't been there, but these clothes weren't what he'd been wearing that morning, when he'd visited the cottage.

He'd been in his old jeans, which he'd changed out of when he'd got home.

But they weren't on his bedroom floor, where he'd left them, and so he ran to his mum and dad's room, flipped the lid of the laundry basket open.

It was empty.

Downstairs the washing machine gave a grumble.

Oh.

*Well, that's that,* he thought, the desperate energy suddenly, simply, sinking out of him, draining away. *That's that.*

His dad had always been rubbish at checking pockets.

That evening, as they ate dinner together, his mum said, 'I've got tomorrow off. We should do something, as a family. It'll be nice.'

'Off?' said his dad.

She smiled at them both.

'Yes, for once. What do you want to do?' she asked, reaching out and almost touching Hex's fat, split lip.

They'd told her the story about falling off the rope-swing.

She'd bought it.

'Tomorrow?' he said.

He hadn't thought that far ahead.

'To the park?' she said. 'Or … maybe to the seaside? We could ask Tommo too.'

Hex's dad looked excited.

'Oh yes,' he said. 'The seaside sounds brilliant. I can make sandwiches and a Thermos of coffee and we'll get some crisps and cartons of squash, and it'll be wonderful.'

Hex's mum laughed, gently, with sheer love.

He was such a big kid.

'For it to be a *proper* trip to the seaside though,' he went on, 'like the ones *I* had when I was your age, Heck, old chap, it ought to start raining just as we're about halfway there, come over really dark and cloudy and just start chucking it down. Then we can have the best kind of English picnic there is: inside a parked car in a car park facing out to sea … a grey sea that merges into a grey sky, which you can't see anyway because of the endless rain … and – *hey presto!* – you've got a memory that'll come back every time you smell that plasticky Thermos-flask coffee smell.'

He was genuinely misty-eyed.

Hex and his mum looked at one another across the table and she rolled her eyes, just like Frank would've.

And Hex laughed. He couldn't help it. They were a family

and there was love here, even if he'd never say it in those words, certainly not out loud.

'Oh, I wish Frank were back,' his dad said. 'She'd love a day at the seaside.'

'Have you met Frank?' Hex said. 'She's *fifteen*, Dad. She'd just find the whole thing *deeply* embarrassing.'

His dad shook his head.

'No, no, old chap,' he said seriously. 'You misunderstand your sister. She would *love* it. I mean, what is there to be embarrassed by?'

And he burped.

'Darling!' said Hex's mum, in mock shock.

'She's *actually* dying of embarrassment in France *right now*,' Hex said, laughing.

'So, it's decided,' his dad said. 'Tomorrow! The beach!'

---

Hex's dad rang Tommo's dad to invite him on the trip.

Hex didn't say he didn't think Tommo would want to come, and neither, it seemed, did Tommo's dad. (Hex didn't know if he'd asked Tommo or just agreed on his behalf.)

Tommo would come round in the morning and they'd all go off after breakfast.

It was a plan they'd put into action a hundred times before.

Everything was normal.

# TUESDAY NIGHT

The glowing digits of the clock on the bedside table said 00:01.

Something had woken him.

Hex flicked the bedside lamp on.

That broke the darkness up into a hundred different shadows.

That was worse, in a way.

He pulled the sheet around him.

What had woken him?

The room was silent.

Somewhere else he could hear his dad snoring, gently, regularly.

The lightbulb slowly grew more confident.

The shadows became more defined.

Behind the wardrobe.

Behind the chest of drawers.

The other side of his clothes on the floor.

The other side of the bed.

A black triangle beyond the lampshade on the ceiling.

The room was silent.

And then a shadow slid out from a shadow and slid across the floor, and up, under and behind the curtains.

He'd *almost* recognised the shape of it, but shadows can be tricky.

There hadn't been anything attached to it to give him a clue.

He thought of that other bedroom, a century before, where Wendy sewed Peter Pan's shadow back on to his feet.

*I believe in fairies*, he thought, just because the words had come, not because he did.

He smiled.

The room was silent.

He climbed out of bed and tiptoed over to the window.

The shadow had gone up behind the curtains.

The window was open.

The curtains moved slightly, just a little waft in the night breeze.

*Shadows don't move by themselves*, he thought, *and if they did I'd be terrified of them, and I don't feel terrified. I just feel like me.*

That meant this must be a dream.

And there's nothing to be afraid of in dreams.

And so he pulled the curtains apart.

It was easy to feel lonely, even when you had friends.

Even when you had people asking you questions, taking an interest in you, because inside each skull there's only room for one.

Hex thought of this as he looked out at the night.

He wondered – then, but at other times too – whether Tommo felt this way. ('Do you feel lonely, Tommo? Like you're the only person who's really real? And you're just stuck there watching the world go by?') But how could you ask a question like that? Not in the daylight, not in the playground, not even on the swings.

Some questions are late-night questions.

Hex wondered what Tommo was doing right now. Whether he was thinking of him.

And then he remembered how late it was.

The night was deep.

The night was dark.

On the pavement a woman was walking a dog.

At this time of night?

And then he recognised – *of course!* – who it was, and Missus looked up at his window then, her face caught in the moonlight, and she waved at him. Smiled at him.

Leafy circled her ankles, a grey great shadow in the night.

'*Come down,*' she mouthed, and gestured with her hand.

And, even though he knew he shouldn't, he did.

***

'You never called,' Missus said.

She sounded almost, but not quite, disappointed.

What could he say? That he'd thought about it, but had lost the acorn? That he *would've* done it, but his dad had put the acorn in the wash?

Or that he'd thought about it, but had decided against it? That he didn't need revenge, after all. That it was only a fat lip and some scrapes and bruises? That his dad had unbuckled the bike wheel, so no harm done, really?

It could have gone both ways. Either way.

He no longer knew.

As the day had gone by he'd been a bottle caught in the river current, bobbing and vanishing and twirling this way and that, yes and no, peace and anger, forgiveness and revenge.

'Never mind,' Missus said. 'I just wanted you to know, I *was* waiting for you. I did wait. I gave you time, Hector. Because I liked you … But … *she* called, and we must answer.'

Leafy rubbed against him.

She smelt of the forest, mossy and smoky and damp.

The air was cool on his skin.

'I'm sorry,' said Hex eventually. 'My dad lost the acorn.'

Missus looked at him, inscrutable in the dark.

Leafy circled them both.

'I always keep my word,' she said. 'I am trustworthy. I wanted you to know that. You *were* wronged, Hector. You *deserved* your revenge too.'

Hex stroked Leafy behind her ear and said nothing, looking at the grey dog.

And then Hex was running, his bare feet thudding painfully on the road.

And Leafy was running alongside him, black tongue flapping and ears bouncing, like this was the best of games.

And before he reached the end of the street Leafy was on him, dog and shadows, shadows and dog, and her mouth of gleaming yellow-white teeth, long and blunt and pointed, glistening in the streetlight that shone on the corner, opened above Hex's face, and her tongue was black and her throat was a tunnel, vanishing darkness, with a pinprick speck of light far off, teasing.

And Hex pushed at her, gripped the stiff front legs in his hands and pushed and rolled, and she dissolved to shadow, to smoke and nothing, and he was free, scrabbling on the pavement with exhausted relief.

'Now, now,' Missus said, walking up. 'Don't fight. We were called, and we always answer.'

'I'll give you *anything* …' Hex blurted. '*Anything* … Just let me be, leave me alone.'

(He heard himself, helpless. His voice thin and weak.)

He was edging backwards, road grit pressing painfully into his palms.

'Let me go,' he whimpered. '*Please* …'

But behind Missus shadows mounted, towered, like wings of night against the face of the night, and from the shadows beneath him, where the streetlight's light couldn't reach, Hex felt fur rising, and even as he let out a cry the dog rose.

Leafy, grey as a fading memory, rose and leapt and flowed and rushed and snapped her shining jaws, surrounded him, smothered him, stole him, took him away … and the street returned to silence.

# WEDNESDAY

Tommo woke with excitement.

He'd slept soundly, deeply, and had dreamt of the day out they were about to go on.

Hex's dad was funny, in an 'I'm glad he's not my dad, but I have to laugh now' way, and he made good sandwiches. He was about as far away from Tommo's dad as you could get.

And the seaside! It'd been ages since they'd last gone there. He could almost smell the fish and chips as he woke up.

He'd been wrong to snub Hex the day before, but he'd felt awful about Sascha's broken arm. Hex *had* been an idiot, chucking those stones around. Tommo shouldn't have joined in, but what was done was done, and now they were off to the seaside.

He rolled out of bed, landing catlike on the floor, and dug around for some cleanish clothes, then headed downstairs.

His dad was in the kitchen, in his vest and pyjama bottoms, leant over the sink, scrubbing at a pan.

'See you later,' Tommo said, as he opened the back door.

His dad grunted something that was barely a word, without turning round, and then Tommo stood there on the back step, looking out at the bright morning, wondering what he was doing.

Everything had fled his mind.

He'd been thinking about *something* … had been about to *do* something … but he didn't know what.

Hex's name and the promised day out that had buzzed in him mere moments before had gone like a dream – he knew there was *something* good, there had *been* something good, but what it was now escaped him entirely.

'I'm gonna go see Jayce,' he said, turning back to his dad once more.

His dad was scrubbing just as hard at the pan in the sink, and still didn't answer.

That was normal.

They didn't always talk much.

He stepped out.

The sun was warm and the air fresh and flavourless.

He took several deep breaths.

He pulled his bike up off the patio and went out through the side gate, meaning to go see Jayce, as he had every day this holiday, but when he pushed down on the pedal he turned the other way on to the street, without noticing.

Five minutes later he was on the doorstep, knocking.

But it wasn't a doorstep he knew.

And the man who opened the door wasn't someone he knew either.

And for a moment he said nothing, just looked at the scene, almost as if he were outside himself.

Then it all came back as if it had never been forgotten.

'Is Hex ready?' he said.

The man gave him an odd look, as if they'd never met before, as if Tommo had never been in this house a thousand times over the years.

'Hex?' he said. 'What … ? Who?'

And then it was all gone again, and the man was a

stranger, not the father of his best friend.

The faint hum of a dream was left drifting smokily in the back of his head.

The world had bounced back to its new normal, again.

'Sorry,' he said, quietly, quickly, nervously. 'Must've got the wrong house.'

He turned away and went back to his bike.

'Um. No problem,' said the man to his back.

As the front door closed, Tommo heard him mutter the word 'Hex?' under his breath.

It was later now.

Tommo and Jayce were at the rec.

They were on the swings, killing time.

They took turns, one swinging, and the other throwing a tennis ball for the one on the swing to kick.

There was a complicated scoring system, depending on where the ball ended up – under the bench, past the roundabout, off the fence …

If you got it *in* the bin, that was top marks, the bullseye.

'And so,' Tommo was saying, 'I asked him if *Hex* was home.'

'What? *Who*?'

'Exactly. So *weird*. It don't even sound like a name, does it?'

Tommo got a good kick in, as he swooped forwards and up, but his mate jumped and, amazingly, plucked the ball out of the air.

'Caught! Out!' Jayce shouted, doing a little dance. 'So,' he went on, 'why'd you do it?'

'I dunno,' Tommo said, genuinely confused. 'It was like I was on autopilot or something. Or like I hadn't woken up proper. But I tell you what, I got outta there sharpish.'

He slowed the swing and they swapped places.

'You're not the only one gone cuckoo,' Jayce said. 'My sister was dead weird at breakfast.'

'Naturally!' laughed Tommo.

He liked Jayce's little sister. She always tried to tell him some new story she'd made up, and pointed forcefully with one of her toys if he didn't look thoughtful and say, 'Very good story, Sascha.'

'No. The other one,' Jayce said, knowing that Tommo was thinking in the wrong direction.

'Maria?'

The older sister.

'Yeah. She was freaking out … grabbed Sascha's arm and shouted about it being fine, like, not broken or something. But, like, real panicked.' He spoke in between powering the swing, higher and higher. 'So weird. I think we'd all know if Sascha had a broken arm. Must've had a bad dream, or something.'

'Weird,' Tommo agreed.

Jayce's big sister was three or four years older than them, and so, except when they'd been little, never really got involved with what they were up to. She had her own friends, and they'd be off in one room, and him and Jayce in another, doing their own things.

Three or four years was enough of a bridge to keep them apart, but sometimes she'd tell them a joke she'd heard at school, or a bit of gossip, and would grumble when they didn't laugh and stomp off and slam her door, and they'd just shrug and say, 'Teenagers!'

Tommo threw the ball and Jayce kicked at just the right moment, and it flew up, away across the rec, and banged into the fence and fell into a shadowy patch of nettles.

'Well, that's that, then,' said Tommo. 'I ain't going in there.'

Jayce began to slow the swing, and when it was just about safe, jumped, landing with a dusty thump and a tumble on the tarmac.

'So Maria's acting strange,' Tommo said. 'Nothing new there.'

'Yeah, guess so. I hope we never become teenagers.'

'Definitely!'

They shrugged and laughed and ran over to where their bikes were, heaved them up, cycled away.

It had been Tommo and Jayce for as long as anyone could remember. The two of them against the world.

They'd met even before nursery. Their parents had lived round the corner from one another and had ended up pushing the kids round the park at the same time. They'd sat at that same rec, chatting about this, that and the weather, while the babies in the prams gurgled to themselves.

Sometimes Tommo would get dropped at Jayce's house by his mum on the way to work, and sometimes Jayce would go back to Tommo's after school.

They half-joked that they'd spent so much time in one another's houses they couldn't remember whose house was actually whose, or whose parents.

There'd only ever been two moments of worry.

First, when Tommo's mum had left and his dad had talked about moving house, but then never did, and second, when it looked like they'd be put in different classes for this last year at primary school, but then a space opened up and they'd both been put in Miss Short's class, together. Although (it was quickly decided) *not* at the same table.

Tommo and Jayce.

Jason and Thomas.

The dynamic duo.

That was them, and they was that.

And that was how it had always been.

Always would be.

🌰

Smoke and squeals peeled off of their brake pads as they came to a halt in Jayce's close.

The trees could be seen over the tops of the houses at the bottom, like green clouds rearing up over a red-tiled landscape of square hills.

Jayce had said, 'Let's go on a *proper* swing,' and Tommo had agreed.

Sascha was sat in the front garden surrounded by a semicircle of toys, reading from one of her many books.

The boys listened.

'… and so the ogre opened up a shop selling postcards, and the witch opened up a shop selling candles, and they lived happily ever after and were never bothered by the happy rabbits again, because they'd all been eaten up.'

'How'd it begin?' Tommo shouted.

Sascha looked up.

'Ah,' she said. 'Boys.'

Then she said, 'Whatcha doing?'

And then she said, 'I'll come too.'

And she put her book down (it was upside down and looked to be one about fire engines) and stood up, wiping the backside of her shorts with her hands.

She turned them over, looked at them, sniffed them, and then said, 'Ah! Lovely and fresh!'

'You can't come,' Jayce said. 'We're going down the woods.'

'Can too,' said Sascha.

'You're not allowed,' said Jayce.

'I'll bring Mr Crocodile,' she said, picking up a plastic horse from among her toys.

Tommo didn't say anything, but he smiled.

(Whenever anyone said, 'Sascha, you can't call it *that*,' about her toys – who were *all* misnamed in the eyes of the sensible world – she would frown and tip her head to one side and say, 'Whatcha on about?')

Tommo admired her, in a way.

When he was little he'd had a stuffed toy, a grey seal, that he took everywhere, called Seal. He wished he could go back and call it something else now.

It had taken Sascha being born and growing up and starting to talk to show him how boring he was, really.)

'Isn't Maria looking after you?' Jayce asked.

'I *was* reading her a story, but she had to go use the *toilet*,' said Sascha loudly. 'I think it might be a poo. We can leave her a note.'

The boys laughed at her unstoppable (unembarrassable!) shamelessness, and the three of them headed off down the twittern between the houses, down towards the rearing green woods.

Beyond the houses the path passed by a red bin for dog waste and a sign from the council saying how lucky everyone was that this copse of trees was still allowed to exist when really the land could probably be better used to build a supermarket or some more houses or a car park.

Stood beside the sign was a woman in a dark grey suit, or maybe a black suit that had just been through a lot. She had greying hair tucked behind her ears and twirled a pair of dark glasses in one hand as she looked at her phone in the other.

She glanced up at them as they passed.

'Morning,' said Jayce.

She stared at him for a moment before responding.

'Yes,' she said.

'We're going to the swing,' said Sascha, swinging Mr Crocodile by its tail.

'Be careful,' said the woman.

'Of course,' said Jayce.

(Tommo tutted inside at the grown-up who felt the need to say something like that. Why did she automatically think they wouldn't be careful on the rope-swing? It was only a little frustration, that being-told-the-bleedin'-obvious, but it made him think of school, and how they'd all be back there next week, sat at their tables, being reminded to wash their hands after the loo and to not run with scissors. As if they didn't already know. A tiny frustration, but still ...)

They walked on.

As they went in under the trees, the warmth of the sun lifted off their shoulders and the cool green air of the woods took hold of them.

He remembered coming this way with Hex and suddenly felt even colder. A memory of a feeling that something had been about to go wrong … time muddled up inside his brain … an old world brushing against the new one …

'Go back,' he said to Sascha. 'Stop following us.'

She stopped walking. Leant her head to one side as if to say, '*Whatcha on about?*'

'What're you on about, Tommo?' said Jayce.

And Tommo shook his head and said, 'What?'

The memory of Hex had gone, the feeling of foreboding forgotten.

'I dunno,' he said. 'It was like that – what d'ya call it? – that déjà vu thing. Like I'd been here before.'

'Course you have.' Jayce laughed, slapping his pal on the back of the head. 'Hundreds of times.'

'Yeah,' said Tommo.

But there was still something at the back of his mind, a shadow of something else that he couldn't quite make out … something else, or some*when* else.

Sascha had started off again, and the boys hurried to catch her up.

As they walked, Sascha bounced around their heels, waving Mr Crocodile and chanting, 'The woods, the woods, they're green and good, bread and pud, oh yes you should!' which, after an uncountable number of repetitions, became a song that Tommo and Jayce sang too, whooping like lost boys on an adventure in the deep forest.

They followed the paths easily, between trees and seas of ferns and nettles, up the slope to the tall oak on the bank above the brook.

And there it was: the thick, rough blue rope hanging from that high branch, dangling a couple of metres above the stream.

Tommo leant on the tree and took a puff from his inhaler. Singing and walking had set his asthma tickling.

As he held his breath for the ten seconds he counted silently, he looked at the rope.

He wondered, as he always did when they came down here, who had set the rope-swing up. That high branch was quite a way up there and he didn't fancy being the person climbing the oak with the wind in their hair, the hard ground just sitting there down below and squirrels getting jealous.

He watched Jayce step out into the brook and grab the tassel of frayed rope that hung below the stick-seat.

He pulled it behind him as he climbed back up the bank.

'Me first,' said Sascha, bouncing.

Jayce, laughing, gently pushed her away as he cocked his leg over.

'Geronimo!' he warbled as he stepped off the bank into mid-air.

And Sascha and Tommo watched with delight as he zoomed away from them.

❦

Tommo didn't often remember his dreams, but there was one that had come several times in the last few months.

He was flying.

He was free.

❦

And then it was his turn and he was flying again, long swings out into the empty air under the green light of the woods.

The sound of the rope creaking above, and the sound of Sascha talking to Mr Crocodile, and the sound of the gentle breeze shiffling the leaves echoed around the forest and around his head.

It was so different to being at school.

There he felt watched from all sides, hemmed in, noticed.

He felt squashed, sometimes, under all the attention, and, like squeezing a bar of soap too hard, he'd slip out of the way and distract the world by doing something daft. It might be pointing out the window at an imaginary UFO, or it might be tipping too far back in his chair, or it might be burping the answer to Miss Short's question.

Even when he was stood outside Mr Dedman's office he couldn't say exactly why he'd done what he'd done, except he knew he'd felt a whoosh of freedom and exhilaration and a momentary release of pressure as everyone looked at him and stopped noticing him.

He didn't mind Mr Dedman too much. He just said words and looked disappointed.

It was when the daftness popped out at home and he got a clip round the ear and sent to his room that he cried. Not for being in his room (he had some comics there and a bed he could curl up on), but for the murky, shadowy, enclosed, stuffy atmosphere it added to.

The buzz of silence.

Compared to all that *nonsense*, the forest was a delirious freedom. It didn't judge him or score him or ask him to explain what his plans were.

But then Jayce was saying, 'Come on! My turn again!'

And Tommo steered the swing back towards the bank and was caught hold of by his pal and pulled up.

He climbed off and Jayce took hold of the crossbar.

And it was then that everything went wrong.

Maria came at them like a meteor.

There was thunder in her eyes and Tommo quaked beneath it.

He'd never seen her like this before, genuinely crazed, cracked, scary, not in all the years they'd known one another.

'What's *he* doing here?' she shouted, glancing and glaring at Jayce, but heading at him.

Dry mud dust puffed at each footstep.

Jayce lifted his hands and said, 'Maria! It's just flippin' Tommo?!'

She didn't seem to hear, and let swing a punch with her right hand that caught solidly on Tommo's cheek.

'You let him near her, *again*?' she shouted.

Tommo staggered backwards, clutching his face, bumping into Sascha, who was stood at the edge of the riverbank holding the stick of the rope-swing in her hand.

Maria shoved him in the chest as Jayce tried to hold her back, tried to put himself between them, waving his arms around and going, 'Stop! Stop!'

Tommo staggered backwards. His foot slipped and he tumbled, and Sascha tumbled over the edge with him.

He bounced off at least one sticking-out root on the way down, and Sascha landed a little way away with a crack like she'd landed on a branch.

She started wailing.

The forest went quiet to let her cry fill all its spaces.

Tommo staggered to his feet, dry mud across his clothes,

his face stinging hot and his stomach lurching its contents up his throat, towards his mouth.

He gagged, choked, swallowed, heaved in desperate breaths.

He didn't have words.

His words had been stolen away.

It had been such a nice day.

It had started weird, sure, but it had been good since then.

He looked up, and there on the bank, high above him, were his friend and his friend's big sister looking down at him …

No, they weren't looking at *him*, of course they weren't … They were looking at Sascha.

They'd turned pale, were frozen like churchyard statues above him.

He was afraid to blink, was afraid to turn round to look at the girl he could hear crying behind him.

And then he did, and the world unstuck and time began to move again.

Sascha was lying a little way away, her arm bent at an odd angle, and she was bawling.

Tommo heard Jayce up above him say, 'What have you done? Go and get help!'

But Maria didn't go and get help. She shouted at Tommo, 'You!

It's *your* fault. It's happening *again!*' and he felt her finger pointing and he heard her moving, heard the creak of roots and scuff of dust and he knew in his stomach that she wasn't coming to apologise.

His world was spinning.

He *understood nothing.*

He clambered to his feet, hurting his hands on stones and thorns, and he ran, as he heard her splash into the stream behind him.

Ferns whipped at his legs and hands as he plunged through them.

Hidden roots and dips reached out to try to trip him.

Trees lurched up in front of him and he swung himself round them.

*What had happened? What was going on?*

His lungs burned in his chest.

*Surely he'd gone far enough?*

Wheezes scratched in his throat, but he didn't pause to get his inhaler out, not yet.

To the side of him, through the mist of his exhaustion, shadows moved, keeping pace with him.

No, not shadows, just one – great, grey and wolflike, and loping easily through and between and around the undergrowth.

His heart drummed in his ears, and he didn't know if Maria was still behind him or if she'd given up, and his face throbbed and his lungs hurt, and he could hardly get a breath in, and he tumbled forward, falling to the ground, not tripping up, just collapsing,

and he found himself rolling on grass, and he lay on his back and looked up at the low dark grey sky above him, and he felt a shiver as the first drops of rain began to fall.

He struggled to draw a breath, shuddering, heaving – his chest so tight, his throat so narrow. He gulped like a sailor reaching for the surface after the ship's gone down.

*Rasp. Wheeze. Gasp.*

The only reason he didn't panic was because he *knew* his asthma, knew it would pass if he kept calm, that it had always passed before … He just needed a quick puff …

(*Why had she done what she'd done?*)

He patted his pockets for his inhaler.

All it would take was one puff, then another, and everything would be back to 'normal'.

He imagined the air quotes as he thought the word, and then the world narrowed around him, right down to him and his rotten, tiny lungs, as he found his inhaler was lost.

*Nothing was normal.*

His pockets were empty.

His heart banged in his chest as panic rose up.

And then, as he gasped and wheezed, grasped for oxygen through snot and tears, something cold and wet nudged against his cheek.

And then a dog was licking his face, licking both his tears and the rain together, with a thick black tongue, but it was warm and it nudged him upright.

It commanded him and he obeyed, still shaking and hurting with each tiny breath he drew, but his heartbeat slowing, the panic receding. At least he wasn't alone. He could get help.

The dog, a huge grey thing, *snurf*ed and snorted and knocked him with its head as it brushed past.

He turned to look where the beast was going and saw the oddest thing.

There was a cottage.

(He knew there was no cottage in the woods.)

There was a clearing.

(He knew there was no clearing in the woods.)

There was a door opening.

(There were no doors in the woods.)

And a woman was coming out, a short, jolly woman who held a shawl up over her head as the fat drops of rain fell.

(Sometimes, he had to admit, you did see women in the woods. But that didn't make the rest of it any less strange.)

'Come on then,' she called. 'Come in, before you catch your death of cold. Leafy'll show you the way, lean on her, boy.'

He was stunned – with the physical hurt, with his asthma, and, further back in him, somewhere almost forgotten but not quite, with the *betrayal* by Maria, who he'd known his whole life.

(Confusion was sinking as unfairness rose.) He was in shock, spun round like a blindfolded kid at a party and left wobbling all by himself while the real world hid.

The woman beckoned again, calling him into her cottage.

'Come here,' she said.

And so, sure that he shouldn't, he did.

<hr>

Inside the cottage it was warm, stuffy even.

A log fire was burning in the grate, and the small windows let just a thin, pale, watery grey light in.

Outside, Tommo could hear the low distant groan of thunder, sounding like a dustcart in the next street.

There was a pair of old armchairs either side of the fireplace and a kitchen over on the other side of the room.

A big oven added its heat to the atmosphere.

Tommo looked around, wiped the rain off his face, felt the pain as he touched his cheek.

His hand came away bloody. Not much, just a blur of red in the rain-wet on his palm.

He wheezed and hiccuped as he breathed, as he tried to breathe.

There was a sticky rattle at the top of his lungs.

The woman gestured him over to one of the chairs.

She fussed off to the kitchen and fiddled with pots and jars.

As she did so, Tommo sat, sinking deep into the soft cushions.

The dog turned round on the rug, plonked herself down and nuzzled her head into his lap.

The cottage smelt doggy, and earthy, but with a cooking smell, like roast dinner, over the top. All very close together.

Tommo ached all over.

He wasn't at his best.

His eyes ran across the ceiling.

It was whitewashed, but shadowy, with just the light from the fire and the small windows to illuminate it. Heavy black wooden irregular beams ran across it from side to side, uneven and ancient.

Between the beams, over by the door, he could just make out a bundle, like there was junk up there, held in place in a net or a sack. The word 'cocoon' came into his head from somewhere, but he wasn't sure if it was the word he wanted. For a moment he thought there were two of them, but then he saw there was just the one, and some pale wisps and threads of torn cobweb beside it, as if there had *been* another one there, but one that was now empty … emptied … And then the woman was pushing a small bowl of something hot into his hands.

'Breathe it in,' she said. 'Just breathe it in.'

And Tommo did.

He lifted the bowl and let the minty, ticklish vapour curl into his nose.

It soaked down into his lungs like water into a dry sponge, and he found he was quickly breathing normally again. The pain eased.

'Oh, wow!' he said. 'That's amazing. Thank you.'

She took the bowl from him and put it on a table, then she came back with a wet cloth and knelt beside him.

She held his chin in her hand and turned his face this way and that, examining the bruises and scratches.

She dabbed at them with the cloth, picking thorns and grit with small precise plump fingers as she spoke.

'So, what is your name, young man? I'm Missus. And she's Leafy.'

The dog had begun to snore gently in his lap.

'Um,' he said. 'Tommo. I'm Tommo.'

'Tommo?' she said.

'Yeah, it's, uh … it's short for Thomas.'

'A good name,' she said, nodding. 'One had doubts, which never hurts, and one was so wise he understood angels.' She said something in a foreign language, her tongue skipping lightly across the strange words. And then she laughed and said, 'And now *you*, the latest Thomas.'

She leant back, put the bowl down.

Tommo looked blank.

He didn't know what she was talking about.

Outside the rain poured.

In one corner it dripped, steadily, into a pan, like a ticking clock.

She got up, poured boiling water from the stovetop kettle into cups.

Made tea.

Came back to the armchairs.

Leafy stirred her grey head in his lap, but didn't otherwise move.

Her eyes were closed, her lips apart, her teeth gleaming yellow, gums gleaming black, and she was dreaming.

Missus pointed at his injuries. The ones on his face and the ones she couldn't see – the bruises under his shirt, the stitch that ached in his side, the continual bottomless tumble of confusion and betrayal and unfairness in his heart that had started when the floor of the good, sunny, happy spring day had fallen away.

'It pains me to see a man brought low like this. One so young given such an unfair drubbing. Needless, unjust.'

She handed him his tea.

Sat herself down.

'Who did this?'

He cradled the cup in his hands.

'No one,' he said.

How could he say it had been Maria? He didn't understand *why* she'd done what she'd done. It felt wrong dobbing her in without knowing why, and yet she *had* punched him, *had* pushed him, *had* watched him fall down the riverbank. He could've broken his arm or his neck or anything … And then he remembered Sascha, and her arm, and her tears.

'They hit hard for no one,' Missus said.

Her eye twinkled mischievously.

Tommo looked away.

'It don't matter,' he said.

'Of course it matters,' she replied quickly. 'Of course it does. If they do this to a kind, gentle boy like you, and are left to go unpunished, then imagine who else they might hurt. Hmm? It's all good and well to be selfless, to be humble and forgiving, Thomas, but tomorrow someone else will have been hurt, and that will be on *your* shoulders, just as much as on those of the one who is doing the punching.'

Tommo shook his head.

'No,' he said. 'That's not right.'

He couldn't be blamed for whoever Maria punched next. Not that he believed Maria was going to punch anyone else – she wasn't like that, she'd never been like that. But now he remembered her eyes, and knew they'd been different to how he remembered them … There had been something else in there, some*one* else, besides the slightly annoying best friend's big sister he'd always known.

'No,' he said again.

Missus leant back in her chair and sighed.

'Maybe,' she said. 'Maybe. But Leafy and I have seen it all before, many times. The world grow worse – darker, colder, more spiteful,

more petty, intolerant, untrusting – all because *we* weren't asked to help.'

Tommo sipped the tea.

It smelt like the staffroom at school.

It needed sugar, but he held it between his hands and let them grow hot.

'She was older than you, wasn't she?' Missus said, after a moment. 'The girl who did this. The one who attacked you.'

'She didn't …' Tommo trailed off. 'I don't know why she did it. It don't make no sense.'

Missus nodded.

'Some people,' she said slowly, 'are born to trouble. It's the bee that buzzes inside them, keeps them moving forward. They might not always mean to cause trouble … but they do. They're driven to it. And they go on, no matter how many people try to point them on to the right path. Hurt. Hurt. Hurt.'

Tommo nodded, without meaning to.

There was something in her words he didn't want to hear.

There was a certain *mirroriness* to them.

He'd been called trouble often enough, and had found himself outside Mr Dedman's door often enough too, and could never explain quite why.

He'd never *meant* to hurt anyone, of course, but sometimes he had.

There'd been that time with Alfie's pee-stained trousers. How he'd got carried away and had run around the playground with them.

'*Why on earth did you …?*' they'd begin, and he'd look at what he'd done and shrug and say, 'I dunno,' and it was the truth, the whole truth, and nothing but the truth.

Sure, he could reach down inside himself and find, say, an answer that went, 'Because I thought it might make people laugh.' And that might be true, but it was only ever an answer to the question he found *after* the event. He hadn't sat there, bored with his book, thinking, 'I know what I'll do, I'll flick this rubber on this ruler and try to get it into Emma P's pencil case.' He'd just done it.

And, it seemed to him, life was like that.

Grown-ups didn't get it. They went on about this thing called 'cause and effect' that meant you had to plan everything in advance before you did it, and show your workings, and be able to say why you were doing it this way and not that—

🐭

'Thomas?' said Missus.

He'd almost nodded off, he realised, lurching up in the chair.

The room was so fuggy, warm and dark.

Leafy lifted her head, gave an enormous black-mouthed yawn, turned round three times and laid herself down on the hearthrug amid the shadows.

'Did you hear what I said, Thomas?' said Missus.

He blinked.

'I can give you your revenge. Get your own back on this girl. This *bully*. This *thug*. Stop her hurting anyone else. If not for *you*, Thomas, then for her *next victim* and the one after that. Think of the trail of hurt you can stop, simply by asking me to help. Asking *us* to help.'

She held her hand out, palm up, to include the dog, Leafy, in her words.

'What are you talking about?' he said.

'She and I have the power,' she said, almost whispering.

He had to lean in to hear her over the noise of the rain outside.

'We can make the girl go away,' she said. 'Make the world forget her. It is simple. No one, not a soul, will remember her, and she will leave no more scars, no more marks. And there will be peace.'

Tommo listened as the words trickled into his ears.

He looked at them one after another and they all made sense, except none of them made sense. It was all mad. This cottage that shouldn't be, this woman who was so obviously a witch out of an old storybook, even the rain outside that there'd been no hint of half an hour before.

But he had to say something.

The moment was dragging on.

The cup of tea between his hands had grown cold, as if he'd sat there for hours.

He wasn't wheezing.

But he suddenly felt a great fear.

'You'd do that?' he said finally.

'Of course we would. It's our role in the world. Setting things right. Making the world safe for the good ones. Like you, Thomas.'

'Yes,' he said, 'I see.'

He was treading water.

He needed to leave but was afraid that if he just stood up the woman would make him sit down again.

And then, suddenly, over the continual susurration of the rain, there came a thud and a clatter.

From inside the oven.

Missus turned and Tommo jumped, dropping his cup.

It bounced on the rug and a dark stain began to spread.

Missus turned back to him and said, 'Oh dear. Dinner's fallen over and you've made a mess. Such is the way of things.'

And she smiled a wide toothy grin that glinted in the orange light.

'What *was* that?' he said, kneeling down and picking his cup up.

Leafy raised her head and looked at him.

'Just the meat falling over. Nothing to concern yourself about. I'll deal with it when you're gone, Thomas. There's a good lock on the oven door. Nothing gets out.'

She smiled again, her eyes in shadow, and Tommo shivered.

She had made a joke.

Had she made a joke?

He stood up, the cup, unbroken by its fall, in his hand.

As he stood he saw, or thought he saw, a movement somewhere above him, up between the black rafters, up in the shadows, but it was nothing, just a cobweb fluttering perhaps, or the bound bundle he'd spotted earlier wriggling. It was too dim, too shadowy under that low ceiling, to tell.

For some reason he had a flash of memory, back to the start of the day, a brief echo of the dream he'd lived – something about going to the seaside with that boy he hadn't heard of. What had the name been? He'd said it when he'd knocked on that door …

And then a shadow crossed his mind and the cottage swallowed him back up.

'Can I get a cloth?' he said, pointing at the spilt tea on the rug.

'It'll soon dry,' Missus said. 'Don't worry.'

And she stood too and placed a hand on his shoulder.

'Come.'

She walked with him towards the cottage door.

Outside the rain was easing up.

'Justice, Thomas. That's what we were talking about. We can do it so easily for you and we ask nothing in return. It's what we came into being for, to provide the balance. Take this.' She pulled an acorn from one of her pockets and placed it in his palm. She closed his fingers over the top. 'Think on what we've said, and if the hurt inside you calls for righting, crush this in your hand and we shall come in the night and smooth the world out while you sleep.'

She opened the door and guided Tommo out with a hand in the small of his back.

His heart pounded.

His legs wobbled.

He felt as if he had just been given a reprieve.

The forest was rich and green before him, damp with the rain that had just let up. Dripping.

He walked between bracken and through ferns, with Leafy beside him, until he was back in the woods he recognised, and when he turned round to watch her go, he found he was looking at the farmer's fields.

The electric fence hummed gently and the wind pushed the rows of green stalks back and forth.

He looked at the acorn in his palm and thought what

nonsense it all was.

And he pulled his arm back and threw it, as far as he could, out into the crops.

Except he didn't.

He tucked it into his pocket almost without noticing.

🐌

Tommo picked his way back through the little copse to the stream, a walk of just a minute or two.

*There* was the rope-swing.

*There* was the riverbank.

And *there* was Jayce, sat at the top waiting for him.

🐌

'Where've you been?' said Jayce, as Tommo stepped across the brook.

Tommo didn't know what to say.

'Sascha's broken her arm. They took her off to hospital.'

'She OK?'

'I reckon so. The ambulance guy said it wasn't the worst he'd seen.'

Jayce tossed Tommo his inhaler.

'It was in the stream,' he said. 'I kept it safe.'

'Ta.'

He gave it a shake and then slipped it into his pocket. His lungs still felt free-flowing.

'Where's Maria?' he asked, looking round.

'Oh,' said Jayce. 'After she came back from chasing after you, she went off with Sascha in the ambulance. She was *really* upset. Even more than Sascha, I reckon.'

Tommo climbed up the root-ladder and sat beside his friend on the high bank, their legs dangling over the edge.

'She's given you a real bash there,' Jayce said, poking at the bruise that was colouring Tommo's cheek. 'Shame we're not at school tomorrow. You'd be a hero!'

'I'm bruised all over,' said Tommo, feeling the aches.

A moment of silence.

Birdsong.

'Where've you been?' said Jayce. 'It's been hours.'

Tommo looked at his watch. Jayce was right. It was practically lunchtime.

'I dunno,' he said. 'I ran. I thought Maria was gonna have another go. And I … I got lost …'

'Lost? In the woods? Not possible.'

Jayce shook his head.

And of course, that was true. The boys knew this small patch of woodland like the backs of their hands. They'd been running along these paths every holiday since they were old enough to run along paths.

'I know,' said Tommo. 'But ...'

And it was just at that moment they realised they weren't alone.

❦

There was a woman walking along the stream-bed.

She was dressed in a dark suit and seemed to be following directions on her mobile phone, which she held out in front of her, like someone with a scanner in a sci-fi film.

Tommo recognised her as the one they'd passed on their way into the woods, the one who'd told him to *be careful*.

She paused below them and looked off away, towards the other, lower bank, and was just about to head up and into the ferns (following the path that he had left?) when she stopped, turned and looked up at them.

She glanced at the screen of her phone, tapped it a couple of times, and then she spoke.

'Ordinary children?' she said.

They said nothing.

It didn't seem like a question you should answer.

She took her dark glasses off and let them dangle in her hand.

Her eyes looked tired.

'Children,' she said again. 'Have you been here all morning?

Since we met earlier, I mean …'

'Um,' said Jayce.

'Er,' said Tommo.

The day was not getting any less weird.

She stepped closer.

'Have either of you,' she said, lowering her voice, 'seen anything *odd* this morning?'

*Where to begin?* thought Tommo, but he said nothing.

'No?' she said, taking their silence as an answer.

'No. Don't think so,' said Jayce, and he shifted where he sat.

It seemed he wasn't going to tell this stranger about his mate going missing for hours in a wood it wasn't possible to get lost in.

Tommo was thankful for that. He didn't want to have to try to explain his morning to anyone. Not before he could explain it to himself.

A pitter-patter of grit and a puff of dust fell down the root-ladder as the boys shifted their feet.

'Very well,' the woman said. 'But if you *do* – any strange thoughts, stray memories, *off* visions … things that don't belong to you – let me know. Ring me.'

She pulled a business card out of her jacket pocket and handed it up to Jayce.

Then she replaced her dark glasses, turned and walked off, crossing the stream with a little hop, and walked slowly into the ferns, towards the electric fence and the farmer's fields, more or less following Tommo's trail.

Before she got too far though, and just as Jayce handed her card to Tommo, she turned back again and said, in a clear voice that reached across the distance with no difficulty, 'I would keep out of the forest, if I were you. There's something wrong here.'

And then she was gone.

Tommo turned the little rectangle of card over in his hands.

It was blank, except for a name, a three-digit number and a logo.

*Mimi Jofolofski*, it said.

There was a crown above the letters DXXA. The Xs were each made of crossed swords.

'After they'd gone off in the ambulance I came back here, to look for you,' Jayce said. 'I was worried. Where have you been?'

As they walked, the story poured out of him.

'It was so weird,' Tommo explained. 'When you couldn't find me … I ran so far, I … I ended up somewhere else.'

'Come off it.' Jayce laughed. But he went quiet when he saw the truth on Tommo's face. 'What did you see?'

Tommo began to tell him about the cottage and about Leafy and Missus, but he'd only got as far as going inside and the magic bowl of steam that'd eased his asthma when they reached their bikes.

'Look,' he said. 'Not a word of this to anyone, right?'

Jayce nodded.

'Obvs.'

Tommo hauled his bike up, heaved his leg over and perched above the crossbar, one foot on a pedal, ready to push off.

'See you tomorrow?' he said.

'Abso-bloomin'-lutely,' said Jayce.

And then, just before Tommo leant into the first downward stroke of motion, Jayce said something else.

'I looked,' he said. 'I looked for you all through the woods. I called and called. You didn't answer. I didn't know where you were. I thought you'd really gone.' He shook his head, his eyes big and shining. 'Don't ever do that again.'

And then he punched Tommo on the arm and said, 'Get going. Watch out for your dad.'

There was a radio playing in the kitchen. The presenter was sharing the news about floods somewhere, a war somewhere else. People fleeing for their lives. Leaving everything behind and fleeing with just the shirts on their backs.

As Tommo went in he saw his dad sat at the kitchen table.

His plate was empty.

The knife and fork lying side by side.

A smear of ketchup like a crime scene.

'Where've you been?' he said, looking up, seeing Tommo in silhouette, backlit in the doorway.

'Down the woods,' said Tommo. 'We lost track of the—'

'Dog's had your lunch,' his dad said, leaning back and pushing his plate away.

They didn't have a dog. His dad meant his lunch was in the bin.

Tommo stood there a moment, breathing.

This was just how his dad was, sometimes. You couldn't be sure which version of him you'd meet when you came in the door, Silent or Stroppy.

This was Stroppy.

But even as he heard his stomach groan his dad's face softened.

He pushed his chair back from the table and leant forward to look at Tommo.

'Christ! What happened to you?' he said. 'D'you fall off your bike or something?'

Concern?

'No,' said Tommo. 'I got punched.'

A frown.

He hadn't meant to say that, and wondered why he had.

'*Punched?*'

His dad came over, gripped his chin firmly between two coarse fingers, and turned his head this way and that.

Tommo wished he'd let go.

He did.

'Who did it? Who've you been fighting?'

'I wasn't *fighting*,' Tommo said. 'I didn't …'

'Who?' said his dad.

Concern, but cold.

'Maria,' said Tommo, 'Maria Peake.'

His stomach lurched low inside him, like a lift suddenly dropping in a shaft.

He hadn't meant to say that, either.

*I've betrayed her.*

It was an odd thought to think, an odd feeling to feel, since *she'd* turned on *him* so unexpectedly, so suddenly, but still something in him looked back at him and shook its head sadly. *You shouldn't have said that. Kids should stick together, not squeal to the grown-ups.*

'Go get washed up,' his dad grunted, pushing him away as he let go. 'I'll make you some toast.'

Tommo sat on his bed and tried to read his comic, but the words slipped past his eyes and the pictures refused to make sense.

He ached all over, not just where he was bruised and scratched.

His dad had shouted up the stairs, 'Listen for the door. There's a parcel coming. I'm off,' and had gone out.

It was always like this.

Had been since his mum had gone.

Just the two of them, rubbing up against one another, like stones.

You were *supposed* to get sparks and start a fire and keep warm, but more often than not, all you got was dust and scrapes and bad feelings.

He thought of Jayce, in that crowded house.

Sure, his big sister had been weird today, but normally she was just Maria …

And you couldn't help but laugh with Sascha. She made the place special, lit it up with a unique imagination. He'd always liked her, ever since she'd been brought back from the hospital as a tiny baby.

Sascha and Jayce shared a bedroom, so (if she wasn't away visiting some friend (and she seemed to have loads, which Tommo found hard to understand, having only ever had the one, really)) she'd often lie on her bed as they played, and she'd tell the stories of the people who flew their spaceships or lived in their castles.

Even Jayce's mum and dad, who argued and swore, even when

the kids were around, weren't so bad. He tried to keep out of the way when they were there, but they always treated him nicely, and offered him the last biscuit in the packet, and never begrudged making him dinner sometimes.

They'd always been like that. Family friends – except they didn't really talk to his dad any more.

He wondered what his mum was doing now. Where she was.

But there was no one he could ask.

And then he woke up, suddenly, when the doorbell rang.

He didn't remember falling asleep, but he wiped the dribble from his cheek and ran downstairs.

The clock said that hours had gone by.

🌰

It was Jayce, and behind him was Maria.

Part of Tommo flinched when he saw her, angry with itself, with her. It huddled him back into the hallway, but then the rest of him, the larger part – the part that remembered years and years of her *not* punching him in the face *really* hard – stepped up and he said, 'Hi.'

'We need to talk,' Jayce said. 'Maria needs to talk.'

He gestured over his shoulder with his thumb.

The girl looked sheepish (was that the word?), as if she didn't really want to be here.

Across the road a pair of pigeons fought over a landing spot, up on the lamp post's lamp.

The flurry of wings and panic distracted them all for a moment.

'Look, can we come in?' Maria said, turning back to face him.

She *was* sheepish (that *was* the word), half anxious that someone might see her here, talking to him. Half embarrassed.

So they went through to the lounge.

Jayce was bubbling with energy, which was the opposite of how Tommo felt. Maria seemed to be teetering somewhere in between.

'Go on,' said Jayce, looking at her and bouncing on the balls of his feet. 'Tell him.'

'Tell me what?' said Tommo.

'She went to the same place as you,' Jayce said. 'Go on, tell him.'

Tommo's heart skipped in his chest.

He sat down on the sofa, sinking backwards, as if someone had pushed him.

Inside he was buzzing.

He wasn't *alone.*

He hadn't had a funny turn.

It had been *real.*

'Tell him about this other boy,' Jayce said. 'This Horace.'

'Hector,' Maria corrected.

She sat down in Tommo's dad's chair.

'It was Monday morning,' she said, as if she were beginning

to read them a bedtime story. 'But it feels like years ago … like another world. I was babysitting Sascha, keeping an eye on her while she, you know, played out front, like she does. But I had a phone call. My … My friend, Hester … She … I …' Maria paused, took a breath, and looked away. 'So I went upstairs, and the next thing I know, when I came back down, she was gone. I was frantic. Looked everywhere. And then, after I don't know how long, *you* came out of the woods, came running up the alley …'

'*Me?*' said Tommo.

'Yeah, *you*,' she said, looking at him. 'You'd taken her. You and that Hector.'

Tommo shook his head.

This didn't make any sense. Monday had been rainy. They'd spent the morning in Jayce's bedroom trying to teach Sascha to play Uno (which Mr Crocodile took more seriously than she did). Maria was playing music in her room, and being shouted at by her mum to turn it down.

He looked at Jayce.

'We were at *your* place.'

Jayce nodded.

'I *know*. I told her. But listen,' he said. 'This is where it gets *weird* … well, weird*er*.'

He was grinning, jiggling … could barely contain his excitement.

'You said Sascha had been hurt,' Maria went on. 'You said she'd fallen, then you said Hector had thrown a stone and hit her … knocked her off the rope-swing … something like that. You were blubbing. Anyway, Dad had just brought Jay home from his swimming lesson, and so he phoned 999 and then we ran to find her. We left him –' she flicked her eyes at Jayce – 'to wait for the ambulance.'

'I hate swimming,' said Jayce. 'I haven't been to the pool for years.'

Tommo knew that. Everyone knew that. Jayce had made such a fuss when he fell in the pond back in infants that he'd been excused ever since. Even standing next to a deep puddle made him antsy.

'You go every Monday,' Maria said.

She seemed certain.

Jayce rolled his eyes and gave her a shrug.

Tommo shivered. A cold shiver, straight up his spine and down again.

He didn't see shadows moving about underneath the sofa, but for some reason he imagined them patiently listening to the words, waiting to sneak up the wall behind him and tap him on the shoulder.

He kept his eyes on Maria.

'She was in the stream,' Maria said, 'and her arm was broken and it was *my* fault. I'd taken my eyes off her. I'd let her get taken. And then this kid started laughing. Up there on the bank above us, pointing and laughing like it was all just some big joke, and I … well, I saw red.'

She flushed as she remembered. Grimaced.

'I went for him,' she said. 'I mean, look, he deserved it. Sascha … she was crying … and he ran off. He was scared of me.' She gave a tiny almost-laugh, something close to a cough. 'Dad was shouting, but I couldn't back down. I'd let Sascha go … and that was *my* fault. Getting him back for her was the least I could do.'

Now it seemed *she* shivered.

She said nothing for a moment, then, 'He ran and I chased him, but I lost him. He must've turned away, turned off the path … or I turned off the path, or … And suddenly I realised I didn't know where I was. The woods were too deep. And there were shadows around me, shadows running alongside me.'

'The dog,' said Tommo.

She stared at him.

'Yeah, the dog,' she said.

'And then the cottage, the clearing,' he said.

'Yes,' she said.

'It was the place you told me about,' Jayce said, breathless. 'This cottage. It's why she's been acting so weird. Listen.'

'What was the dog called?' Maria said, giving her brother an angry-ish sidelong glance.

'What?'

'The grey dog that led you through the woods.'

'Leafy,' Tommo said.

'Oh God,' said Maria.

'What did the woman say to you?'

'She talked about feuding families, like in the Wild West … how someone shoots the kid of one family, and so that family kills the kid of the other, and then it goes back and forth. Eye for an eye, and tooth for a tooth. She said I was *right* to be angry, that I was *right* to want justice. That I was *right* to protect my sister, to defend her, to *avenge* her …' Her voice was snappy, coming in bursts. 'I felt sick at what I had done. I was supposed to be *looking after her*. But it was *his* fault she fell, it was him who threw the stone … and Sascha, you know, she's too small to get her own back, she's just a little kid … so it fell to me to protect her now, after I'd failed before … so I took the deal Missus offered.'

'An acorn,' Tommo said.

She looked at him now.

He couldn't make out the exact look in her eyes, whether it was fear or sadness or anger.

'Yes,' she said.

'You crushed it?'

'I did.'

Jayce looked from one to the other.

'I changed the world,' Maria snapped. 'I changed the world. And now I don't know where I am. That *stupid kid* …'

'Hector?'

'Yeah, he *made* me do it. He kept rubbing it in, what he'd done … what he'd done to Sascha … I couldn't stand it. And she *forgave* him!' She gave a nasty little laugh at that. 'I couldn't think of anything but getting our own back, and she just laughed it away. And she's not changed. Which is about the only thing that hasn't.'

'Slow down,' said Tommo, trying to follow her breathless words. 'What's changed?'

'*Everything.* Jay's scar from when he fell on to the fireplace when he was five is gone.'

'What scar?' said Jayce.

'Mum and Dad are … different, they're not quite the same. Different haircuts, clothes … Little things. And my bedroom carpet's a different colour, the curtains are … Stuff like that … and …'

She deflated.

Ran out of words.

Ran out of batteries.

Fell silent …

A clock ticked.

They all breathed.

'Tell me about this Hector,' Tommo said after a moment, changing the subject.

'No one remembers him,' Maria said.

'I didn't know him,' she said.

'Only what I'd heard from Jay,' she said, nodding at her brother.

'Don't look at me,' said Jayce, lifting his hands.

'You weren't in the same class as him,' she said. 'But I remember you coming home sometimes with stories of what he'd done. He was one of them show-off kids, always doing daft things to get attention. All "Me, me, me", but stupid with it. I remember he grabbed some kid's trousers once,' she said, 'some poor sod who'd peed himself, and he ran round the playground with them. A right little bully, it sounds.'

Tommo felt his stomach fall away.

'That was *him*,' Jayce said, pointing.

'It was meant to be funny,' Tommo muttered. 'Just a laugh.'

'We watched the nativity play at your school once,' Maria went on, 'and right in the middle of Mary's big speech, one of the sheep did an enormous fart and fell over dead, with its feet in the air. That was him.'

'Nah, that wasn't Hector, that was …' Jayce began. 'Oh, what was his name?'

Tommo racked his brains too.

'Tall kid, white hair, smelt cabbagey, moved away in Year Four …'

'Odo. Odo Parnell.'

'That's it.'

'One more thing about this Hector. He was best mates with you.' She looked at Tommo as she said it.

'Nah, that's *me*,' said Jayce, slapping his chest. '*Always.*'

'Always,' said Tommo reflexively.

'I remember it differently,' said Maria, shaking her head, tense and crackling. 'I come from a different world now. Or I'm *in* a different world now … I don't know. Mum used to keep cactuses, but now there's not a single cactus in the house. And we've got a different brand of toothpaste. Why the hell's all *that* changed?'

Tommo believed her without a second thought. He knew what Missus had offered. She'd had this Hector removed, like he could have *her* erased, and the world had *reshaped* itself to fill the gaps. (And it bounced and echoed along the way. He could remember remembering, but couldn't remember exactly what he'd remembered about this other, missing, kid …)

'Must've been something to do with Hector,' he suggested. 'Maybe something he did when he was five … Maybe he was in the garden centre, over by the house plants, and you were there too and so you went to the cactus bit instead, to avoid him, but then that didn't happen this time round.'

He started thinking about the ripples and changes. What was different about the original Tommo, that one that was mates with Hector? He'd been a different person, in a different time too.

It was a lot to take in, but somehow it was a nonsense that made sense. *This* – he looked around at his home – wasn't how things were meant to be.

Outside the house, gravel crunched under the wheels of

a car and an engine went silent.

'So what do we do?' Maria asked, almost frantic. 'I'm stuck here.'

Her eyes, when she looked at Tommo, sparkled with tears, and she was afraid.

'She gave you one too,' she said. 'An acorn.'

Tommo nodded slowly.

'Is it for … for *me*?' she said. 'Because I punched you?'

He nodded again.

'Tommo,' she said, stepping towards him, just as the rattle of a key looking for the lock came from the front door. 'Whatever you do—'

'Quick,' Tommo hissed, leaping up. 'Go out the back.'

Maria and Jayce looked startled, puzzled, afraid, frozen in place.

'He knows you hit me,' Tommo hissed.

And with those words, and with the *shnick* of the key finding its way home, and turning in the lock, they understood, and Jayce led the way out into the kitchen.

Tommo went into the hall, pulling the lounge door shut.

'Do you need a hand with anything?' he said as his dad wrestled his key from the lock.

'What?' he grunted.

As he slammed the front door, Tommo heard the careful distant shutting of the back door.

'Out the way,' his dad said, pushing past him, going into the front room, switching the telly on.

Tommo stood where he was, his head spinning, his heart racing, from both the close call and Maria's revelations.

He took a breath.

And another.

Touched the unmoving hall wall with one fingertip.

He was falling down a long drop and he just knew he hadn't reached the bottom yet.

# WEDNESDAY NIGHT

That evening Maria climbed out of her bedroom window.

She stepped out on to the garage roof and clambered down the fence into the driveway.

At least her escape route was still here, in this new world. It wasn't, after all, the first time she'd snuck out after her little brother and sister had gone to bed.

The sun still rose in the east and sank in the west, and the prime minister was still the same one, and the wallpaper in her bedroom was still the embarrassing unicorn pattern she'd picked when she was nine and that they'd never got round to replacing. But so much else was different.

She hardly recognised the people she lived with.

That had been a shock, waking up the morning after Missus had done the deed. Hearing her mum *humming* as she made coffee, humming a happy little jingle, as if nothing had happened.

Her cheek had still stung with the injustice of that slap and she'd been ready to snap back at whatever sarcastic thing her mum said, but she'd walked into a different-looking kitchen, filled with *happy* parents, who weren't angry with her.

It was only slowly though that she'd begun to understand what had happened, to accept the truth, to actually believe that the woman in the woods had been real, that her promise, her *deal*, her *magic* had all been real too.

Ripples.

In that dark little cottage the woman had said the world would heal around the absence, once she'd snipped that stupid boy out of it, that, like a wound, the sides of the world would come back together and it would be as if he'd never been.

And part of that healing was *change*.

Maria was the only one who remembered how all the world had been before.

She stalked up the road in the twilight, her heart following along behind her, dragging itself at a desperate distance. It refused to talk to her, after what she had done.

●

It had only been a couple of days, and the hurt still stung.

It was embarrassment, partly, and shame.

She had *turned away*, had gone indoors for a minute, two minutes, maybe, when she should have been with her sister. Her little sister. Her daft and defenceless little sister.

Sascha was pure and innocent and didn't see danger in anything.

And when Maria had come out and found *no Sascha* there, she'd run around the close and looked in the house and under the car and had driven herself mad. Her heart had kept beating-repeating, 'This is *your* fault, *you* did this, *you* didn't care enough,' and it was right.

If anything happened to Sascha it would be on her, *forever*.

What her mum and dad would say wasn't a part of her thoughts, not right away.

But they would *never* forgive her.

And so, after the initial burst of frenzy, she'd gone up to her room, had called Hester back, listened as it went straight to voicemail. And she slumped, sat on her bed, staring at the carpet.

If she stared hard enough, she'd thought, maybe she could

convince the world it had been a mistake, that Sascha *wasn't* missing. That in a minute she could go and look out the window and she'd see her sister sat on the lawn, waving Mr Crocodile around.

Her head had buzzed.

But her heart had whispered, 'That won't work. She's gone, and everyone will blame you.'

She'd tried not to breathe, tried not to hear.

Missus hadn't erased *this* hurt.

And then, when the boy had come running up and banged on the door Maria had felt a surge of relief. Anger and relief.

It had been someone else's fault.

The anger was pure and sharp. Had found a focus.

She set aside her own shame and replaced it with blame.

This *Tommo*, this *Hector*.

They had taken something precious and had crushed it, ruined it, broken it, hurt it, hurt it, hurt it.

Sascha.

Poor, quirky, beautiful Sascha.

She knew she'd get her own back, would have her revenge.

Violence was the easy, obvious – and justified – answer, but the world had grander ideas.

She'd found her way deep into the tangled woods, into the shadows, into the witch's hut.

Missus's deal didn't let her forget *this*.

◦

Maria looked up and found that she was outside Hector's house.

The night had descended around her as she'd walked, and it was dark now.

She'd known this was where she was coming, where her feet were leading, even if she didn't exactly know why.

She'd only been here once before, in that other, earlier world.

Her cheek stung, even though the mark had faded away, even though her mother, this new one she was having to come to understand, wasn't the sort of woman who'd ever slap her daughter.

She was lost, a stranger in a world that looked the same.

She was alone here.

All because Hector had got himself deleted.

The anger had drained away.

Yes, it had been *his* fault. He'd *deserved* the beating she'd given him, but …

But it should have ended there.

It was her *mum*'s fault for pushing her over the edge, for stoking the anger, for *making* her summon Missus and Leafy. Right here,

on the pavement outside Hector's house.

Her mum's fault, but … but her mum didn't remember doing it.

Who was left to blame?

She pushed the doorbell.

A man answered the door.

'Hello?' he said. 'Yes?'

Light spilt from the hallway. The warm smell of a late dinner. Distant music.

'Mr Patel?' she said.

'Yes?'

'I'm sorry,' she said, holding her hands out, palms up. 'I didn't mean for it to happen … for it to go so far.'

'Um?'

All she wanted was for things to go back, for this weight, this solitary burden of knowing, this responsibility that no one else knew about, to be lifted. She wanted to be forgiven, but they didn't even know what she'd done, and yet she saw it everywhere she looked. She wanted things to go back, or to be allowed to forget, to join the new world herself, as everyone else had.

And then she said the boy's name, and the man's face, this man who had been Hector's dad in a different world, almost flinched.

'Oh my God,' he said, not upset like she was, but gently surprised.

And then he stepped back into the hall, into the light.

'I think you'd better come in,' he said. 'There's someone you ought to meet.'

Inside the front room a woman was standing, examining the ornaments on the mantelpiece.

She was not much taller than Maria, with greying hair tied back in a bun and wearing a scuffed black suit that looked like it had seen better days.

Tommo lay in bed on his side, looking at the strip of light that crossed his bedroom floor from the open door.

The telly was on loud downstairs.

Sometimes he was surprised the neighbours didn't knock on the wall, or the door.

He was spinning everything round in his head.

Grown-ups talked about how the days sped up as they got older. How they flew by compared to when they'd been kids. Miss Short sometimes said this, and she'd get a wistful look in her eye and go all quiet for a moment, half mucking about, but also half obviously real.

Tommo couldn't wait for time to speed up. Days could be so

long, and today had felt like the longest day.

What with everything that had happened, the fight that wasn't a fight, the flight through the woods, the whole business at the cottage, the long ride home … the afternoon's conversation, the empty hours alone after Jayce and Maria had gone …

The knowledge that he had been someone else in this other world, this other *timeline* … that he'd been friends with this Hector there, and not Jayce, that he'd run for help when Sascha had broken her arm, even though she wasn't the almost little sister he loved to laugh with. In that world … he'd done a Good Thing.

That thought made him smile.

He would've done the same thing now, of course … except he hadn't had the chance.

He wondered what this Hector had been like, besides the things Maria had said.

He wished he remembered more than the occasional dream-like feeling of this déjà vu.

Hector sounded like a bully, like a show-off, like an annoyance, but Tommo was sure that wasn't the whole story.

What the world saw, and what happened inside (inside the skull, or behind the front door – both were private places the public didn't see into) … he knew these were different things. Oh, sometimes they might be the same, or sometimes *mostly* similar, but sometimes the two faces, the *you* you showed and the *you* you saw in the mirror were as different as snow and fire.

In time Tommo fell asleep, his head spinning with a constellation of possibilities.

He woke up in the night and lay in the darkness.

The landing light was off.

There was silence in the house, broken only by the regular rasp of his dad's snoring.

But then he heard something else.

Outside.

In the alley.

The window was ajar because the night had been warm again.

A cool trickle of air crept under the curtains.

A soft scraping sound, like fabrics rubbing together, or a cat rubbing against your ankle.

He dipped his head under the curtains.

The moon was full, and hung high up in a starless sky.

The alley was pitch-black below him.

Except at its mouth, where it met his street, over to the left.

There was a lamp post there that cast a yellowish light, a narrow triangle of which edged into the alley.

He heard the sound again, somewhere below him.

Shadows rubbing against shadows.

The night sliding past itself.

It was very late.

As he looked out at his street, beyond the mouth of the alley, the streetlight went out.

Darkness engulfed everything, but then slowly, as he watched, a fuzzy greyness took its place.

The parked car across the way, the metal pole of the lamp post, the shallow edge of the kerb, the shape of a person.

He blinked, and there was no one stood there.

A bird beat inside his chest.

There was no one there, just the shadow of a tall dog slinking away round the corner, out of sight.

And then a crack, a buzz, a hum, and the streetlight flickered back into life.

It had been Leafy, hadn't it?

Grey as night, whiskered with fear.

Waiting for him to call her.

For a moment, not pulling his head back from between the curtains, he thought she was in the room behind him, and he couldn't move.

Tommo was under his covers now, rolled up and facing the wall in the dark.

Silence. (*Snore.*)

Just silence. (*Snore.*)

And in the silences between snores he remembered, or imagined, or remembered imagining, or imagined re- membering, being the Tommo from *before*. The Tommo who was friends with … Hextor? … no, *Hector* … instead of Jayce.

What Maria had said made him feel like he'd seen a trailer for a behind-the-scenes show about some movie, a glimpse of scenes before the special effects were added … but it was only a glimpse, no more.

He'd been shown that how things were now weren't necessarily how things *had to be*.

He wondered what the Jayce in that other place had done, who *he'd* been friends with. Maria hadn't said, just that they were in different classes and didn't know each other.

And that led him to think about Jayce – his best friend. His forever friend. And how, in a way, he didn't really know him at all.

*Is Jayce thinking of me right now?* was a question Tommo could never know the answer to. And this wasn't him being soppy, wanting the attention or to know his friend cared. This was a basic problem with the universe, he thought, with the world, this inability to ever know, even when you're sat in the same room, whether you were in someone else's thoughts.

(How real *are* you if no one thinks about you? If no one remembers you?)

He'd tried to say this, to explain the knots and confusions the questions tied him up in, but no one else seemed to feel the same trouble, or they simply didn't understand.

(It was perfectly possible to have friends and still be utterly lonely.)

And so Tommo lay in the dark and wondered.

These were the sort of thoughts that kept him awake at night. (They were a distraction from thinking about how he'd upset his dad that day, or where his mum might be, or what *she* might be doing … or whether she ever thought of him … or … Oh! What was the point?)

It was a distraction to focus on the tiny mysteries of mind and body. (He knew his fingernails were growing, for instance, but he only noticed when they were long and snagging on things, never the in-between. So he tried to notice the in-between, and wondered what it felt like, *growing*. He knew it happened *slowly*, of course, so what if he slowed himself down, so that a day outside seemed like a minute inside … Would he feel them growing then?)

(Tommo didn't know the word 'philosophy', but in bed, in the dark, it knew him.)

Jayce woke up in the dark.

A car door slammed somewhere in the street, and there were hushed voices, and then the sound of Maria climbing, almost silently, up the fence, and creeping across the garage roof.

*Well,* he thought, I *wonder where she's been?*

But then he fell asleep again before the thought could worry him, and dreamt of adventures that mixed his comics with films and with the woods, and they were light and funny, and when he woke, later, still in the dark, he remembered nothing of them, except that he was smiling.

And he lay there for a while, listening to Sascha breathing, so loudly for a girl so small, and it was all perfect, not that he'd ever admit that to anyone, and he smiled again before falling into more dreams in which he was the hero.

# THURSDAY

Tommo opened the fridge and looked in.

There was a milk bottle in the door, but no milk.

There wasn't much else in the fridge either.

The house was quiet.

His dad hadn't got up yet, and on days when his dad didn't get up, you tiptoed.

There was only a crust of bread in the breadbin, and Tommo's stomach rumbled.

A hot chocolate and a slice of toast wasn't too much to ask, was it?

His face was tight and hot, where the bruises and scratches stretched, and his ribs ached.

Waking up, he'd wondered if the day before had been a dream, but the pain proved to him it hadn't. It had all happened – *all of it*.

As he counted the money in his purse, he thought about the thoughts that had played in his head. About all the possibilities – the other Tommos, other Marias, other Saschas in the other worlds. About how he could never know what they had done, what they'd thought, how empty their fridges had been … What had the Tommo in the world before had for breakfast? Who'd been waiting for him in the kitchen?

He felt light-headed, dizzy with the thoughts he only half-understood.

As he went out the back door he eased it closed behind him, as gently as he could.

Even though it was a warm day he pulled his hoody up.

🌰

By the time Tommo got to the shop, a couple of streets away, he had rolled the ball of possibility around in his head so much he wasn't sure what to think any more.

Maria had changed the world, she said. She had described all the things that had changed after this other kid, this, oh …

Hector! (even now the name was slippery, and fell out of his head if he didn't concentrate on it) … had been 'removed'. The world had flowed like water to fill the gap, making little changes here and there … changes you couldn't have predicted.

He looked at his life and wondered two things. What had it been like before the changes Maria had set in motion (something she couldn't help him with, not having known the other Tommo)? And what might it be like if things changed again?

In his pocket was an acorn, a trigger he could pull that would remove Maria and set the world in a new direction. The last fourteen-odd years would be different, from Maria's non-birth to now, but what would that mean for Tommo? What would that do to his friendship with Jayce, and what would it mean to his mum and to his dad?

He didn't know, of course. Couldn't know. Couldn't even guess.

He stepped into the cool of the shop, automatic doors parting to let him through, and he walked over to the chiller cabinet to get a bottle of milk.

As his fingers hooked into the handle a voice called his name.

🌰

Sascha held out a marker pen and lifted up the plaster cast, and said, 'Be the first, Tommo.'

Behind her, Mrs Peake was holding a basket, and looked like

she was about to tell Sascha off, before she saw who it was the girl had run up to.

'Thomas!' she said.

'Hi, Mrs Peake,' he said, trying not to meet her eye.

He knelt down with Sascha and popped the cap off the pen.

'Look, it's classic white,' she said. 'I saved it for you, because it's because of you I broke it, and it's only fair and right you get to write first. Right?'

'I'm glad we bumped into you,' Mrs Peake said. 'She's been on about this since she came back from the hospital yesterday. It's driving me mad. Well, madder.'

She reached out and pushed Tommo's hood down.

'Are you all right?' she said. 'Jason said you slipped and fell.'

She examined the bruises and scratches.

'That's quite nasty,' she said.

'It's OK,' said Tommo, twiddling the marker pen between his fingers.

'Did your dad take you to get looked at? You could've chipped a bone or something. Concussion, if you hit your head. Jason said you wandered off?'

'No,' said Tommo. 'I'm OK. I'm sorry I left her, but I had to get home. I knew she'd be OK with Jayce.'

He was muttering, stumbling over his words.

His head spun.

'Come on,' said Sascha, poking him in the ribs.

'Well? What shall I write?' he said.

Mrs Peake straightened up and said, 'I'll just be over here,' pointing at the cheeses. 'Glad to see you're OK, Thomas.'

He breathed a sigh of relief that she was so … incurious.

He lifted Sascha's arm and wrote 'Hope you're Arm is Better soon. Love, Tommo. x'.

A black car was parked a little way up the street from his house. As he passed it, the door opened and a woman climbed out.

She stopped him with a hand on his shoulder and said, 'Are you Thomas Roberts?'

He stepped sideways and shrugged her hand off, but then he recognised her. It was the woman who'd been acting strange in the woods the day before, the one who'd given Jayce her business card.

'I'm Agent Jofolofski,' she said, 'and I need to talk to you. It's important.'

She was serious.

And she was the police.

And she'd been in the woods.

'OK,' he said. 'But quick, yeah?'

She invited him to sit in the car, but Tommo refused (she might be police, but you still didn't get into cars with strangers – he wasn't stupid), so they stood together on the pavement.

'I spoke with Maria Peake,' the woman said, pulling an old-fashioned ring binder out of a bag and laying it on the bonnet. 'She filled me in on some of it.'

'Maria?'

'Yes, she turned up at the house of a man I know. Well, I know his daughter, and she'd asked me to pop in and speak to him. He'd been remembering some unusual things he couldn't explain, and so had she. She'd woken up yesterday believing she had a *little brother*, and she even remembered his name, but when she mentioned him to a friend they said, "Who?"'

She started flicking through the pages inside the folder.

'I've known her for four or five years,' the woman went on, 'and she's never had a brother in all that time. But just that morning we'd had some odd readings on some of our equipment. There was evidence of an Unauthorised Temporal Reweave, overnight, some strange ripples in the Undercurrent.'

Tommo looked at these unfamiliar words.

'Temporal', he knew, was something to do with time, like 'temporary' or 'tempo' … And 'Reweave'? Well, he knew what 'to weave' meant – it was like knitting or something – so to *reweave* must be to do it again …

*Time had been remade.* He already knew that, of course.

And 'Unauthorised' was easy enough. It was written on the staffroom door.

This woman, Agent Jofolofski, was saying she had equipment that had detected what Missus and Leafy had done.

'Undercurrent?' asked Tommo. 'What's that?'

'It's the name we give to the level of reality beneath ours, the bedrock in which the world we live in is planted. We have ways of sensing certain disturbances in it. It happens from time to time,' she said. 'We get these readings, like ripples on a pond, like a stone's been dropped through reality, or pulled out, and the water's rushed in to fill the gap … But normally we've no idea what's changed. People have their déjà vus and they have their misplaced memories or mistaken identities, but usually we can't pin it down. This time Ms Peake has been able to help fill in the facts for us. It's been years since we've been so lucky.'

'Who are you?' he said. 'Are you really police or what?'

'I told you,' she said. 'I'm Special Agent Mimi Jofolofski, and I'm with the Department of Extra-Existent Affairs.' She smiled at him as she said it. 'We deal with the … unusual.'

'OK,' he said.

'Ms Peake gave me your name, told me where to find you. But the man I mentioned, the father of the girl I know, he also mentioned you.' She looked him up and down. 'His description didn't mention these bruises, but was otherwise quite accurate.'

Tommo realised who she meant.

'I knocked on his door … yesterday morning.'

'And asked after your friend. This "Hector".'

'Yes.'

'You were caught in an echo of the previous time,' she said.

Tommo nodded.

'He was my friend, Maria said. She said we were best mates, not me and Jayce … not me and her brother, but …' The story began blurting out of him.

Special Agent Jofolofski was a grown-up, and she was talking to him as if he were one too. She was treating him seriously, and that felt strange and powerful. She wasn't treating him like a child, like a daft kid who flicked bits of eraser at Megan Greenberg when they were supposed to be doing a maths test. And although he knew he *was* that daft kid, he was also this *person* talking with a secret agent about proper weird stuff, like an adult.

'And I can't stop thinking about what it might've been like … before …' he said, 'and what else might've been different and how many times has this happened and …'

'Slow down,' she said, with half a smile. 'The *what ifs* are always interesting, but it's my job to protect this country against them. Against beings that can change our history on a whim. And Ms Peake said you might be able to save us.'

'Save you?'

'Save *us*.'

'How?'

'She said you've been where she went and you were offered the same deal as she was. But, I'm guessing, you haven't *completed* it yet?'

He put the milk down on the pavement and carefully pulled the acorn out of his pocket.

'Oh my,' she said. 'I've read reports, but I've never seen one in the flesh.'

She took a mobile phone out of her pocket and held it up to the acorn, tapping the screen and making *Mmm-mmm* noises.

Patterns and waveforms flashed across the display.

'It's definitely from *somewhere else*,' she said. 'It's quite amazing.'

She tucked her phone away and looked him in the eyes.

The acorn sat in his fingers between them.

'Would you like to save the world, Thomas?'

'Um,' he said. 'I guess.'

'Good,' she said. 'Now, look at these for me.'

She pointed at the folder that sat on the car bonnet.

In clear plastic sleeves, one on top of the other, were pictures.

She slowly flicked through them.

They were all pictures of cottages in clearings.

'Look close,' she said.

Some were blurry photographs, others were woodcuts, like from an old book, some were detailed drawings, and at least one was the sort of little kid's drawing you might've seen stuck to a fridge.

None of them were the cottage he'd seen. He felt sure of that.

'The quality's not always great,' Agent Jofolofski said. 'There's only been one encounter in recent years, since people started carrying camera phones.'

She turned to a nice clear colour photo.

This cottage had pale plaster walls and was bathed in sunlight. There were skulls around the door frame.

'Not that one,' he said.

She flicked to the next picture.

It was in black and white. A really fine ink drawing, or perhaps an engraving, and it was just right. The clouds were beginning to drizzle overhead, the well was in the right place, the windows were just as he remembered them, and there was the shadow of Leafy lurking, just off the edge of the image.

He shivered.

'That's the one.'

She nodded, and pulled the photo out of its plastic sleeve.

'Good, that's what Ms Peake said too. I needed to check we were all on the same page, you understand. Make sure we're talking about the same enemy.'

She paused, and looked hard at the photo, as if she were trying to wish herself into it.

'This, Thomas, is a Vengeance Elemental,' she said. 'Last reported a century or two ago, in a forest up north. It's quite a nasty one.'

'What's a –' he tried to get the words right – 'a Revengeance Element … ?'

Agent Jofolofski spoke as she tucked the photo back into the folder and put the folder back in the car.

'You know what a parasite is? Yes?'

Tommo nodded.

'I think so,' he said.

'A parasite is a creature,' she went on, 'that lives in or on another creature and takes what it needs to live *from* them. Like a leech sucking blood from your leg, or a tick sucking blood from your arm, or an oneirovore sucking your dreams from your pineal gland. What we have here is an Elemental Pocket Dimension, an EPD, doing much the same.'

'The cottage?' said Tommo.

'The cottage, the woman, the dog – it's all one creature. Think of them like its hands and mouth and eyes … The EPD's the whole thing – like a spider in its web, if the web were actually part of a spider, which in a way it is … an extended sense organ.'

At the words 'spider' and 'web' something tickled in Tommo's mind, some memory of something he'd seen, but the woman kept talking, and he didn't have a chance to snag hold of the thought as it went past.

'The woman,' she was saying. 'Did Ms Peake call her *Nemesis*?'

'Just Missus,' said Tommo.

'The woman, this Missus lady,' Agent Jofolofski went on, 'is the bit that talks to you, like a mouth. And the dog is the bit that bites you, like a … mouth too, I suppose … Hmm. And the cottage … well, maybe think of that as the stomach where the person they take, the soul they snip out of the world, is … digested.'

'Hector?'

'In this case. According to Ms Peake. But none of that is what the EPD *really* looks like, that's just how they appear to us little humans … how our brains interpret what is actually something far stranger, something that exists *outside* our world. I think of them like leeches, latched invisibly on, its body a little pouch dangling outside reality.'

Tommo gulped. He'd been in there, in the stomach of this *thing*, and he couldn't help but hear the words that Agent Jofolofski had said a little earlier, about saving the world, rattle around in his ears. He had a bad feeling about this.

'Each time the EPD feeds, our world is changed. The universe is elastic,' she said. 'We can detect that a change has happened, but we usually don't know if something's been cut out or if something's been added in. As I said, this time's different. Ms Peake has told us about Hector Patel.' She paused for a moment as if double-checking she'd said the right name. 'Each time the EPD feeds, a whole timeline is erased … rubbed out and rewritten. We in the department have sworn an oath to stop this sort of interference. Only, *we* can't go where we need to go to stop it.'

Three sudden thoughts jostled in Tommo. The first was: *Why is every change bad? What if what's rewritten is better than what was rubbed out?*

The second was: *Things can be removed from reality and things can also be added in.*

And the third was: *She needs me to go back to the cottage.*

'I need you to go back to the cottage,' Agent Jofolofski said quietly.

She rested a hand on his shoulder.

'OK,' he said, and then, immediately, wondered why he'd agreed so quickly.

She had got something out of the car. It was a small metal disc.

She handed it to Tommo.

'We need to detach the EPD from our reality, unhook it … but the only way to do that is from the other side, from *inside* it. And I can't get in there. You need an invitation, and Ms Peake, having fulfilled the deal she was offered, has worn hers out.'

'But I haven't?'

She shook her head.

'And so you should be able to find the way back through the woods. It will assume you want to talk again, I expect, to bargain or ask it for more. You should be able to just walk up to the door.'

'And then what?'

'Flick the switch –' she showed Tommo a small button on the disc, hidden under a sliding cover –

'leave it by the cottage, and get out of there. It's on a five-minute delay. Don't wait any longer than that, or …'

He stood and looked at the device before putting it in his pocket.

'When it goes off, it will push our realities apart, sending this leech, the EPD, off in a direction we can't see … *away*. Oh, eventually it'll reattach somewhere else, on this world or another one, of course, somewhere in the future. But you can save our world for now, Thomas,' she said.

'For now?'

'*For now* is the best we can ever do. There's always another threat round the corner, but we face it, deal with it, and then we face the one after that … It's what it means to be human, Thomas, dealing with the problem in front of you.'

He nodded.

There were all sorts of thoughts in his head. Chasing each other. Tripping each other up.

He needed time to sit down and put them in order, to look at them properly, but for some reason he didn't feel scared by the prospect of returning to Missus and the cottage. In fact he wanted to go back there, had already been thinking about it, because he had questions he wanted to ask her.

But whatever happened, he was just a kid, and he knew he'd've never been able to summon the courage to go back to Missus by himself, following his own plan. He'd've doubted everything too much, been too unsure of his footsteps at each turn, second-guessing each decision … but the way Special Agent Jofolofski spoke to him, the way she treated him as if he were a normal person, not a kid, was … what? Surprising? Pleasing? Emboldening?

All of those.

'I won't let you down,' he said.

She looked at him, and didn't blink.

She nodded.

Perhaps almost smiled.

Tommo blushed, turned pale, turned away, kicked at the kerb.

'What about Maria?' he asked, after a long moment.

'Ms Peake?'

'Yes. Is she … in trouble?'

Special Agent Jofolofski scratched her temple and sighed.

'In trouble?' she said after a few moments. 'She consorted with an Illegal Supernatural Entity to erase not just an individual, but a whole associated timeline. She has destroyed uncountable possible futures, Thomas … Uncountable unknown possibilities were snuffed out the moment she agreed to do this EPD's business. Who knows what this Hector might've become, or might've influenced, or inspired, or discovered.'

'Poor Maria,' whispered Tommo.

'Of course,' Agent Jofolofski went on, 'the only proof of this is in Maria's memories. Our world never knew Hector, has no record of him, and doesn't miss him. And consequently, there is no proof that a crime has even been committed … A few ripples on a scanner, a few odd memories … So I have no cause to arrest her. And besides, having talked to her, I think any punishment I could mete out would be peanuts next to living with what she has to live with.'

'Is there nothing you can do? To help her, I mean?'

'Oh, I'll keep my eye on her, but …'

She stopped speaking, leaving the sentence hanging there, and suddenly Tommo felt time rush in upon him.

How long had they been talking?

He had to go.

⁂

As soon as he opened the back door the silence hit him.

His dad was sat at the kitchen table, staring at nothing.

Tommo lifted the milk bottle up and said, 'I got milk.'

His dad said nothing.

'And bread,' Tommo added, letting the loaf dangle from his other hand.

After a long moment he put the bread on the table and turned to open the fridge.

'You shouldn't go out without telling me where you're going.'

'Sorry.'

There was silence again.

Tommo stood staring at the little light in the fridge, feeling the cold air on his face, smelling something left too long in the salad drawer.

A little later his dad came up to his room, leant round the door and told him he was going out.

'I've got to see a man about a dog,' he said.

'You're to stay here,' he said.

'Don't wander off again,' he said, 'and don't answer the door, not for anyone.'

Tommo was sat up on his bed, back against the wall.

He had been playing a game on the console, but he was finding it difficult to concentrate.

It wasn't his dad interrupting that caused him to die.

'OK,' he said.

'Good boy.'

And so the day went by, slowly, quietly and endlessly.

The conversation with the special agent – he'd had a conversation with a special agent! About saving the world!

Him! – circled in his thoughts, of course. How could it not?

He could sneak out now, go to the woods and do as she asked.

But if his dad came home and found him gone, again …

He was afraid of what would happen, in a way that he wasn't afraid of returning to the cottage. (Oh, he was afraid of Missus, especially now he knew what she was, but she was something from a nightmare or storybook, whereas his dad was really real.)

So he stayed home.

He had some toast at lunchtime.

He held the acorn in his hand.

That little thing that could change the world.

The world he was supposed to save.

Could it change his dad?

Could it change his mum? Could it find her, somehow? Turn this into a world where she stayed?

Such a small thing, this out-of-season acorn.

He'd go tonight, when his dad was asleep.

He closed his hand over it and just held it.

# THURSDAY NIGHT

The day had been long.

The world was still strange, and Maria kept finding little differences that threw her each time.

Things were kept in different places, were different colours, all that.

It wasn't just her brother who had different friends, but so did Sascha.

A stream of them came by the house that afternoon, each

wanting to look at her arm in its plaster cast, and each of them expected Maria to know their name. Each of their parents spoke to her as if they'd met before, and she had to keep pretending.

It was exhausting.

From what she'd learnt, her own friends had shifted too. Some of them were the same, but some weren't.

The ripples that had come from Hector's removal seemed odd and random.

Things had shifted in the school, in the classes, in the people he'd known and met, and that affected who their brothers and sisters had met or knew. Jay having different friends meant that her family had been swept into a different orbit. So now they knew Tommo's family, but they didn't know Victor and Wynn's. Jay didn't remember them, and it seemed they might not even be at his school in this version of the world.

It gave her a headache.

It gave her a dark cloud.

The responsibility pushed her shoulders down and made her heart feel like a fish gasping on a mudbank.

She sat in her bedroom with the door closed.

She didn't even know if the homework she'd had over the holiday was going to be what the teacher wanted when she handed it in on Monday.

And she'd looked at the address book on her phone again and again, searching for Hester's name.

Late that evening a car drew up in the close outside, and her phone buzzed.

It was Special Agent Jofolofski.

Maria climbed out of her window, as she had the night before.

'He's going to the wood. I'm here to keep you safe,' the woman said.

'Safe?'

Maria was sat beside her in the passenger seat.

'In case something … goes wrong.'

They were both looking out the windscreen.

'In case he decides to rub me out, you mean?'

The woman turned, looked at the girl's face.

'He may not mean to,' she said. 'But if it comes to that, I can protect you.'

Maria didn't turn to face her.

'I would deserve it,' she said.

Special Agent Jofolofski began to say something, and then stopped.

The two of them stared out into the night as the streetlight above them flickered, crackled and went out.

Behind them shadows rose from the dark back seat.

It was a quarter to midnight and Tommo wasn't asleep.

He'd had extra squash just before bed and had lain there for hours needing to pee, unable to fall asleep because of the pressure on his bladder.

He hadn't wanted his alarm clock to go off, in case it woke his dad.

He slipped out from under the duvet, into the dark.

Shadows brushed against his ankles as he walked across his room.

It might've been the carpet.

(He was already dressed. Had been since before he went to bed.)

He tiptoed down the stairs, clutching the banister, stepping over the creaky step, and crept into the hall.

He used the downstairs loo, but didn't flush it.

He went on.

The shadows of the furniture in the front room welcomed him as he walked through.

They bowed as he passed them, the narrow shaft of light from the lamp post outside shining a dagger blade between the curtains.

Into the kitchen.

He put his shoes on there and tried the back door.

It was locked, of course.

The key was in the … No, it wasn't in the lock.

That was unusual.

He looked around in the greyness for the key. Patting the kitchen table, the work surfaces, with his hands.

Nothing, nothing, nothing … and then he knocked a beer bottle with his wrist and he heard it wobble, topple, clatter on the worktop … the hard-edged sound of it rolling … and he flustered, fluttered his hands around, and he touched it just as it reached open space and fell, smashing on the tiles of the kitchen floor.

Darkness held its breath.

His heart paused.

The shadows cocked their ears to listen to the silence.

There was a creak upstairs.

A thud.

Then the silence of a large man moving sleepily across a room.

A grunted call.

Tommo hurried.

The key wasn't anywhere it should be, but he had to go, and so he ran through the lounge and into the hall.

His dad was at the top of the stairs.

'Tommo? That you?'

There was a grumble to the words, but a soft sleepiness too, as if they weren't quite awake yet, just like the man who had said them.

Tommo said nothing.

He had to do this.

He reached the front door, turned the catch and opened it.

And he slammed it behind him.

Pausing for a second, he could hear the hollow thudding of footsteps down the stairs.

Then he ducked to the side, round the back of the house, through the gate.

He heaved his bike up off the patio and was pedalling even as he went back through the gate and up the path.

As he passed the corner of the house a dark shape loomed out at him and they almost collided.

Tommo wobbled, but the bike kept going, out on to the pavement, as his dad fell back against the front door, tripping, stumbling, and grabbing at the frame to stop from falling.

He pedalled, bouncing into the road between parked cars, and off into the night.

Behind him was just baffled, angry shouting.

At the end of his road, he turned on to the bigger road that ran downhill all the way to Jayce's close and the woods.

He paused there, just past the corner.

Now he could hear nothing behind him.

The shouting had stopped.

His dad had given up the chase.

How much did he care that his son was running away in the night?

Enough to come out the front door, but not enough to run up the street.

*Middling*, Tommo reckoned.

It could be worse.

(He imagined he could hear the *flap, flap, flap* of his mum's slippers on the tarmac. She'd've chased him further, wouldn't she? She'd've caught up with him, and wrapped him in a hug that drove away the darkness and the dark thoughts. Wouldn't she?)

He flicked his bike light on, and set off once more.

The dark was the darkest he'd ever seen.

The headlight on his bike lit a small white patch before him. It wavered as he wheeled the bike along the path.

Beyond that little bike-light puddle, which flickered and wobbled, he simply couldn't see a thing.

Something rustled off to his left.

An animal moving?

A hedgehog running away from the noisy human?

Or something more malevolent watching him?

He left the bike lying by the trickling stream and crept forward, up the bank.

Something brushed his face.

The slightest of ticklish brushes, like the faintest fingertips of a ghost.

(Oh! Why did he have to think of that?)

He climbed to his feet and tried to steady himself.

(*Ghosts aren't real*, he thought. *They're just stories to scare little kids. They're not real.*)

The darkness was no longer complete.

Some patches were a darker darkness and some a slightly less dark darkness.

Above him there were patches of lighter darkness that might be the sky through breaks in the canopy.

The forest before him was a patchwork of dark greys, and slowly, with his hands in front of him, he stepped up the gentle slope of the bank, aiming for the darkest shadows.

In his pocket he felt something move.

The acorn called to him, shifted slightly against his leg.

And then he stepped into the black.

A hundred thousand stars shone.

A great sweep of them from one side to the other, with swirls and clumps and spinning patterns breaking off and rejoining even as he watched.

The cottage was lit dimly by this starlight.

The windows glowed orange from within.

Shadows watched from the woods as Tommo moved closer.

Damp-tipped fingers of mist brushed his ankles.

He stood outside the cottage door. Wondered if he should knock.

He moved to the side, over to one of the windows.

Knelt on the bench below it and peered in.

It was hard to see what was happening at first.

Missus was sat at the kitchen table.

Behind her the oven hunched, wide and metal, the dull glow

of cooling embers inside.

She was leaning over something.

It looked like the remains of a feast.

There was a torn-off end of a loaf of bread, bowls and knives.

A goblet and a jug.

And in the centre of the table a roast *something*, like you'd see at a medieval banquet, a whole animal, far bigger than a chicken or turkey or leg of lamb. A whole *something*, with patches of meat carved away so you could see the white curves of ribs.

The candlelight flickered, and it almost seemed to move as the shadows played across it.

Missus reached out with long fingers and, sliding the knife into the cooked flesh, removed a strip, a dangling strip of meat, and lowered it slowly into her mouth.

And she shuddered as she sat there, staring at the ceiling, eyes closed, face flickering in the orange light.

(At the back of his head, on the inside, a sudden wash of memories that weren't his: *a Christmas long ago … sandcastles revealed by a lifted upside-down bucket … tall trees swaying above him … a reflection in a window looking out over the sea of a face that wasn't his face.* Whatever she was eating, these memories were leaking out from it – from *her* – as she swallowed.)

He looked at the oven, at its dull, persistent glow of embers, and suddenly he shivered, with the chill of the night, the reality of the adventure he was on, the foolishness of coming back to this place.

She wasn't … *good.*

He shouldn't be here.

But here he was.

And he had a job to do.

He could leave Agent Jofolofski's device on the window sill.

Press the button.

Go back the way he came.

That was what he should do.

Do what she had asked and get out of there.

That would be him saving the world (he'd probably get a medal or something) … but that would mean saving *this* world.

The one where he lived the life he had always lived.

But could he do better than that?

That was what he had been wondering, thinking about, considering, ever since his conversation with Agent Jofolofski that morning. (Had it only been that morning?)

He pushed open the door and stepped inside.

It was warm in there. Cosy.

Leafy was on the floor by the fire, gnawing something like a long bone dripping with meat.

Missus looked up from the table.

She wiped her mouth with her sleeve and blinked wildly.

(Another faint, distant whirl of memories-that-weren't-his tickled the back of his mind: *watching telly as a family … curtains drawn against the winter … daft sit-com … and a hot chocolate before bed …*)

'Thomas?' she said, standing up and stepping towards him.

Her teeth were pointed and pale in her wide smile.

Leafy dropped the thing she was chewing and pulled herself on to her feet.

'What are you doing here?'

Behind her, tiny shadows fluttered across the table, pecking at the feast.

Tommo felt sick.

Above him there was the faintest of movements.

He looked up and saw that the cocoon-like parcel was still there.

'I expected you to call on us,' Missus said, stepping closer, hand outstretched, 'but not to come calling. Why *haven't* you called us?'

Tommo backed up, feeling the doorknob against his spine.

'I had to ask you a question first,' he said, watching the words come out of his mouth. They sounded steadier than he felt, even if the little whistle of a wheeze came with them. 'A couple of questions.'

Leafy pushed her wet snout into his hands.

'I'm all ears,' said Missus, with a blank face.

Tommo had rehearsed this all evening, had run the questions round in his head all night.

'You changed the world—'

'No,' Missus interrupted. 'The world changed itself. It heals itself, backwards and forwards. Time is the great healer, as they say.'

Tommo wiped his hand on his hoody, put his hands in his pockets.

Leafy turned away, circled, turned back and sat.

She was huge, and stared at him with eyes that were endless.

'Who was I before?' he asked.

Missus said nothing.

'In the world with Hector in it,' he added. 'You remember it, don't you? You know who I mean? You know who Hector was?'

Missus said nothing, but her eyes flickered up.

Tommo looked at the bundle suspended between the rafters.

(Did it wriggle? Ever so slightly? Ever so slowly?)

His heart pounded, slower and slower.

She had just confirmed what he'd suspected. His plan would work.

(Agent Jofolofski had said 'like a spider', and Tommo knew spiders caught their prey and stored it for later.)

His breath wheezed gently, a calming tickle.

'The Tommo, the *me*, from before …' he asked. Pause. 'Was he … Was he happy?'

Missus took a step closer and reached out with her hand.

She touched his cheek with the back of three of her four fingertips, as a mother might.

'I don't know,' she said. 'I was there, yes, but I didn't *notice* you. I spoke with Hector, but he never *mentioned* you. I know nothing of who you *were*.'

Again, her eyes flickered up to the ceiling. She just couldn't help herself.

'If we change the world again,' he said, stepping round her and into the cottage, away from the door, 'can you know what will change and what will stay the same?'

Missus turned to face him.

She cocked her head on one side.

Leafy flowed silently behind him.

'You want to know … ?' She paused. Tapped her tongue between her teeth. Looked behind him. 'If you would be … ?' She paused again. Tilted her head slightly. Leafy snuffled. She listened carefully to things that Tommo couldn't hear. 'We remove the girl who hurt you. And then, fourteen years ago, she's never born. Instead her parents' first child is a son …' She tilted her head and listened. Winds Tommo couldn't feel whistled softly through the room, at the very edge of his hearing. 'They call him … Jason, like the great hero of old. He is not the boy you know. You never meet him.

You have other friends instead, your parents …' She stopped. 'The possibilities the world could follow become *so very many* by then, little pebbles falling, trickle-down to landslides beyond my sight …'

He nodded.

He couldn't *know*. That's what she was saying. But he had to take the chance.

Any new world couldn't be as bad as this one, could it?

Any new world would shake the dice, would shuffle the cards, would deal him a new hand.

And Agent Jofolofski had said that we can't always tell if something has been removed or if something's been added.

He trusted her, because she trusted him.

He had to force a change.

He was lonely, in that house that balanced between silence and violence, walking the tightrope every day. Oh, the loneliness might step aside at school or with Jayce, but the moment the front door closed, it rose up. It was a part of him. It was the part that waited and watched and welcomed him into its arms.

He liked Jayce, he loved Jayce, they had great fun, so often, but that didn't stop, couldn't blot out, the feeling he always had that he was alone.

What was Jayce thinking now?

What was he doing now?

Fast asleep, dreaming, probably.

It seemed so simple to be him, and so difficult to be Tommo.

'Give me him back,' he said, pointing at the bundle.

Missus cocked her head, looked from him to the ceiling.

'Give. Him. Back?' she said.

'Hector,' said Tommo. 'Let me take him back to the world, back home.'

'He is mine,' Missus said coldly. 'I made a deal, and I was called upon, and I claimed what was mine.'

Tommo was ready for this.

His heart fluttered like a butterfly trying to escape, his stomach writhed and his legs felt like jelly, but he had an answer.

'I was sent with this,' he said, holding Agent Jofolofski's device up. 'Let me take Hector back and I won't set this off.'

Leafy rubbed against his leg, lifted her nose and sniffed at the metal disc.

Missus leant in and peered at it.

'It's made of iron,' she said. 'I can smell that, but it's been a long time since that's been a threat to us.'

'It's a sort of bomb,' he said.

(He'd hoped she'd recognise it and be afraid, and screech, 'Take him! Anything! Let us be!' But she'd barely glanced at the device.)

'A bomb?' she said. 'A child comes to us with a bomb and attempts to make a new deal? We like a deal, true. But this is not a trade we care to engage in.'

He slid the little cover back from the button and hovered his finger over it.

'All I have to do is press the button,' he said, 'and you'll be blown up … No, not exactly blown up, but, well … sort of, detached from the world … unhooked …'

He was stumbling over his words and he knew it.

The moment that should have been heroic was fumbled.

He'd been stupid to come here and try this, stupid to think that he could outwit some monster from beyond space and time.

Agent Jofolofski had been wrong to trust him, and he'd been wrong to not just do as she asked.

Why had he tried to push further, to make his own plan?

Why rescue this boy he'd never met?

He wouldn't get that old world back, Maria's world.

He had his world, the world he'd always known, and that was where he was meant to be, and now he had a sudden dread feeling that he wouldn't even have that.

Sinking.

Missus prodded him with a bony finger.

'I made a *deal* with you, Thomas, but you have *insulted* me by returning and *demanding*. I offered to do good for you, to help you stand up to those who *threatened* you, and yet you come here and *threaten* me.' She paused, hissed, prodded again. 'Unlike a *little child*, however, I am able to defend myself. I do not need to turn to others for help.'

She flipped her hand so that a long fingernail pushed at the soft flesh between his chin and throat, and behind him he felt Leafy growing darker, bigger, colder.

The cottage grew dimmer and shadows clustered to watch, and Tommo took an instinctual fear-driven step back, his heart alarm-clocking in his chest, and he slipped, tripped and fell, crashing to the floorboards.

He had dropped Agent Jofolofski's device as he fell, and heard it thud and clatter and roll away across the stone floor.

But had he pressed the button?

He didn't know.

And then the thought was driven from his mind as he hit the floor, and a sharp, sudden pain in his hip, an intense, focused hurt, stabbed into him.

He realised it was the acorn in his pocket – that hard nodule of nut, pushing through flesh against the bone – and as he rolled he knew he had cracked it.

The acorn had been broken.

The deal was done.

The contract completed.

The moment the acorn was crushed, Leafy howled.

'It is time,' Missus said, suddenly ignoring the fallen boy.

*Howl!*

'The night is deepest, let us claim what is ours. I hunger.'

*Howl! Howl! Howl!*

And as Tommo looked, they both faded from sight, like ghosts blown on a summer breeze.

'Oh!' he said as he slowly climbed to his feet.

He looked up at the bundle hanging between the rafters.

This was his chance.

Was the bundle wriggling more now?

He reached out with his hand, but couldn't reach it.

*Something to stand on?*

(How long did he have, how long before Missus and Leafy returned?)

The only thing was the chair at the kitchen table.

He took a deep breath – there was a tickling, ticking wheeze – and went over there.

He tried not to look at the meat on the table.

He tried not to let the delicious trickles of roast-dinner smell enter his nose … the faint memories like the *feeling* of having read a story, but forgetting the details, leaking from the meat.

He pulled the chair with him, letting the screech of its scrape across the flagstoned floor shatter the silence, and placed it under the bundle.

He climbed up and tugged at the thing above him.

It was sticky like spider's web, but covered so tightly that he

couldn't see inside.

It was even more obviously person-shaped now he was close up.

His fingers could hardly pull more than a few strands of the substance away with each scratch … *This will take forever!*

He jumped down and ran back to the kitchen.

Found a wicked sharp knife.

Climbed back up.

The shadows around the cottage watched, intrigued.

Something like this had not happened once in ten thousand years.

Carefully, carefully, he poked and probed and prodded with the tip of the blade in between strands of thick webbing.

It began to cut, and beneath them he could see the hint of cloth.

He cut further, faster, while trying to be careful … cutting along the edges, away from whatever was inside (was it really what he hoped –

*who* he hoped?), and with each slice the cutting became easier, the thick, sticky threads sliced simply and dangled away, wafting in the unfelt wind … and the cloth-covered thing inside bulged out of the opening gap.

Tommo's heartbeat, drum-like, echoed in his chest.

His breathing, asthmatic, whistled in the dark.

His hand shook.

It was hard, working at the thing above him.

His arm ached.

His neck ached, looking up.

His cheek ached, swollen from Maria's fist, suddenly throbbing.

The body inside bulged towards him, threatening to fall as soon as he'd cut enough of the supporting strands away.

He hadn't thought about this, but before he could begin to plan—

*Plop!*

The thing fell.

On top of him.

Knocking them both to the floor.

The knife went skittering, spinning away across the stone floor, ending up swallowed by a shadow under one of the armchairs.

Tommo cracked his head as he fell and the world went black.

'Tommo?' said a voice.

Groggily he came to.

The world spun.

The back of his head throbbed. Stabbed pain as it touched the stone floor.

'Tommo.'

Someone had hold of his shoulder and was shaking him.

'I thought you hated me,' the voice said.

'I thought you'd given up on me,' the voice said.

'Mates forever,' the voice said.

And then Tommo felt something wet hit his cheek.

A raindrop.

A single salt raindrop.

And he opened his eyes.

The world swam, but above him, dark in silhouette against the orange glow of the fire, was the face of a boy.

'Hector?' Tommo said.

'Hex,' the boy replied, correcting him. 'Only Mum calls me Hector, you know that.'

'Huh,' said Tommo.

He tried sitting up, but his head throbbed when he did.

'Ouch,' he said.

'You came to rescue me,' said Hector … Hex.

'Something like that,' said Tommo, staggering to his feet.

He didn't recognise the boy in front of him. Was sure he'd never seen him before. Not the faintest memory flickered. But still, it *was* Hector. He *had* rescued him.

'We've got to go,' he said.

'Uh, OK,' said Hex.

Tommo couldn't be sure if this would work.

He did it without thinking because, the truth was, you could *never* know, however hard you plan … You could never be sure you were doing the right thing.

If he could take Hector back to the world, everyone had said time would change to fit him back in. *Everything* would change again.

It was only then, as they were about to leave, that Tommo remembered Agent Jofolofski's device.

He'd dropped it when he fell.

He'd heard it roll away, even as the acorn had jabbed him in the hip.

Had he pressed the button?

They stumbled to the door.

Pulled it open.

'I remember this place,' said Hector. 'But the sky …'

He trailed off as he took in the roof of stars above the clearing, spinning and shining unlike anywhere in their universe.

Even as Tommo pushed Hex forwards ('Run,' he said), out of the cottage ('I'll follow,' he said), towards the woods ('I'll be right behind you,' he said), he looked back (ready to run in, find the device, press the button for sure) and … shadows rushed together in the middle of the cottage.

They heaped up on top of one another, like insects, like clothes on his floor, like kids piling on in the playground …

And then they faded away, vanished into the orange glow of the room, and there stood Missus, and there stood Leafy, and between them, lying on the cold stone floor, was Maria.

'Are you still here, Thomas?' said Missus.

He was stood in the doorway.

Maria wriggled and scrabbled and fought, even as Leafy, crouched above her with long spider-legs of shadow like curved cage-bars, wove her web and bound her arms tight and tighter to her sides.

'Tommo,' she gasped. 'Run for it. Get out of here. Look after Jay and—'

Her voice was cut off as her mouth was covered.

Missus looked down at the girl.

Leafy didn't stop.

Maria was rolled back and forth as more webs wrapped round her.

'Let her go,' said Tommo.

He wanted to run into the cottage and rip at the webs as Leafy spun them, rip them off Maria and drag her out of the cottage, into the clearing, away from the monsters.

(*Never mind finding the device,* he thought, *just get her free.*)

Missus stepped towards him, placing herself between the boy and the captive.

'You asked me for this, Thomas. Just minutes ago. It's too late to back out now.'

'It was an accident,' he said, a wobble in his voice that echoed in his legs. 'I didn't mean it.'

Only grunts and groans came from Maria, but still she struggled.

Missus took another step towards him.

'Feeling selfless, are you? Going to trade yourself for her?'

Mockingly.

(*At least* Hector's free, he thought.)

'OK,' he said. 'If that's what it takes.'

'You would stay here, with us? If we let her go?'

She held her hand up, and behind her, Leafy paused.

Tommo heard the scrape and strain of Maria wriggling on the floor.

(Her foot hit a chair, which squealed away, then fell clattering on the flagstones.)

A sharp-toothed smile spread across Missus's face.

'We can talk about it.'

'Let her go first,' he said. 'Please.'

Missus stepped aside and looked at her dog.

'Loosen a few of the bonds,' she said. 'Let's hear what she has to say.'

A flicker of shadow, and the webbing across her mouth was slit, and with a gasp of breath it fluttered aside.

'Run, Tommo!'

He took a few steps towards her.

Knelt down beside one of the armchairs, the dog and the girl before him.

Missus rested a hand on his shoulder.

He could feel the nails.

He steadied himself with a hand on Maria, the other on the floor in the shadow of the armchair.

'You would trade yourself for her?' she said. 'After the things she did to you?'

A finger flicked up and tapped at the swelling around his eye.

'Truly a saint.'

Mocking.

'Don't do this,' Maria said. 'I deserve it after what I did.'

Tommo looked at her.

Shook his head.

He could see her eyes, in the gap between two strips of white-grey web. They were blue and scared and beautiful.

*Get scared later*, he told himself. It was something he'd read in a book once. *Easier said than done*, he added.

He trembled.

*I'm not getting out of this, but at least Hector's free.*

'It's all right,' he said quietly. 'I've set things right. I've put the world back.'

'What?' Maria said, her voice almost a whisper.

'Yes,' Missus said, leaning close, echoing Maria's question. 'What?'

'But I can't leave you here by yourself,' Tommo said. 'I've seen what they do. You've got to go back. We …'

As he whispered those words, he felt heroic, like he had made a difference, like he was that kid you see, all dirty and grimy and in the darkest of holes in the last bit of the movie, who suddenly turns it all around.

His hand was in the shadows under the armchair, and as he had talked he had searched, and his very fingertips had found the cold silver blade of the knife.

As he spun it, so he could grasp the handle (whether to fight the witch or to free Maria he didn't know), Leafy looked up …

… and she growled, and Missus looked up at what the shadow-dog had seen, tilted her head like a crow.

'No,' she said. 'That's not right.'

They were looking at the empty cocoon.

'What have you done?' snapped Missus, pulling him to his feet with that clawed hand that was still clutched on his shoulder.

The knife clattered as he stumbled up.

She spun him round, thrust him across the room, towards the kitchen, towards the oven.

He staggered backwards.

Banged up against the table.

'You can't go round invading people's homes,' Missus said, jabbing him with a black fingernail. Darkness rose behind her like wings. 'Stealing their things. It's rude. It's wicked. It deserves punishment. It is a *wrong* committed on us which deserves *righting.*'

Her voice was calm again now.

Smelt of peppermints.

'Tommo,' Maria said. 'Thank you for trying. I'm sorry I hit you.'

'That's OK,' he said, leaning to the side, to look past Missus at the web-trussed girl on the ground. Leafy growled over her, hackles up, a pointed paw resting on her side. 'I'm sorry it's not gone better.'

She gave him what he thought was a smile.

She rocked back and forth as she spoke, like a caterpillar trying to work out the limits of its freedom.

Leafy backed away, snapped at her, growled, spun shadows.

'Tell that woman, the secret agent, "Thank you" too,' Maria said breathlessly as she writhed. 'She tried … to protect … It's not her fault it didn't work out.'

And with that she gave the mightiest wriggle, and rolled away from the dog, thwacking her bound feet into the back of Missus's legs, sending the witch staggering to the floor, hands out to stop her fall.

'Run!' Maria shouted.

And Tommo did.

And Leafy howled.

I *tried to save her*, he thought. *To save us. I tried my best, but I'm no hero …*

He lay on the hard, cold ground outside the cottage, the dew on his lips, a wheeze rasping at the top of his lungs, and the paws of the great grey dog on his back, and he thought again, I *tried*.

Leafy's teeth gnashed by his ear, her breath dripping hot and damp on his cheek.

And then Agent Jofolofski's device, which had been biding its time all this time, counting down, underneath the armchair, next to the knife, did whatever it was it did.

The first thing Tommo noticed was that the weight of the dog, of Leafy, vanished from his back.

He rolled over and half sat up.

Ahead of him the cottage door was open, and the grey dog was falling into it, as if she were falling down into a deep pit, as if he were sat on the side of a precipitous slope.

Beyond the door, inside the room, a ball of darkness grew … darkness with a pinprick of bright sunlight at its centre.

And Missus's face glared up at him as Leafy fell past her, and he backed away on his bum, up the slope, across the stones, along the path, towards the trees.

He couldn't see Maria, but he knew she was still in there, and he cried, 'I'm sorry,' out loud, again and again.

She'd saved him.

And the ball of darkness grew, and the walls of the cottage bulged inwards, and the straw of the thatch crumbled down, as if it were a black hole growing in the middle of that cosy-but-evil building.

Above and behind and before him, the stars spun, wheeling skies full of stars.

And then there was nothing and he was falling.

Leaves whipped his face and branches slapped him as he fell, and his nose was filled with the scent of the forest, and all around him the world stretched out senses and fingertips of possibility to fit itself into the new facts, and to fit the new facts into it.

Time walked itself back to new beginnings and the distant stars spun untouched and untroubled.

# FRIDAY

There was birdsong.

 And there was the smell of ferns unfolding.

 And there was the feel of dry mud prickling his face.

 And Tommo woke up.

The sun was high up, flickering at him through the leaves of the trees that grew all around.

His head was muggy with thoughts that didn't quite fit, that didn't quite make sense.

Falling.

Deep dreamless sleep.

Falling.

And then he was here, in a forest.

No longer falling.

Looking around, he could only see trees, and the sea of ferns his head was poking out of.

His sides ached, the bruise on his face was still there, his lungs wheezed reassuringly.

He was the same boy, as far as all that went.

The forest smelt beautiful. Not of roasting meat, but of openness and freshness and unstoppable green.

From somewhere the rumble of a tractor came to his ears.

And then a robin began shouting from a nearby twig, vigorously repeating, 'Get orf moi land!' in its own tiny language.

He climbed to his feet.

He was wobbly, but that was because he'd just woken up. After a few steps he felt more normal, more secure in himself.

Then he heard shouts.

Pushing his way through the undergrowth, Tommo headed towards the sounds.

Raised voices in the woods.

Whoops and cheers.

And laughter.

He reached the brook, and before him, high up, loomed the great oak, and from it the rope-swing he knew.

His bike was nowhere to be seen, but there, soaring above him, was the boy he'd seen in his dream the night before …

No, it hadn't been a dream.

And he called up, 'Hey, Hector!'

And the boy looked down from the motionless moment at the top of a swing and said, 'Oh, hey … um?'

And then he zoomed away, back towards the bank, where a girl stood waiting for him.

A girl of about their own age.

Tommo watched as Hector landed on the bank and the pair swapped over.

The girl climbed on, and with a loud 'Geronimo!' launched herself into space.

Tommo made his way round, avoiding her legs, and clambered up the bank to stand beside the other boy.

'You made it back then,' he said.

'What?' said Hector.

A look of strangeness, of suspicion.

'Oh,' said Tommo.

'It's Thomas ... Tom ... isn't it?' said Hector. 'You're in Miss Short's class, ain't you?'

'Yeah,' said Tommo.

It seemed unnecessary to ask if they were friends, because clearly they weren't. It had taken this Hector a while to place him, to place his face. *Just some kid he's seen at school.*

But, like one of those daft time travellers you see in the films, Tommo felt compelled to ask the one question ('Say, *what year is it, mister?*') that would get him strange looks: 'Say, do you know who my friends are?'

Hector gave him the strange look he deserved, but before he could answer, the girl landed on the bank, done with swinging, and Hector reached out and grabbed the rope, so she could dismount.

'Hi there,' she said, looking at Tommo.

He half-recognised her, but couldn't place her.

(Then he realised he *had* seen Maria's face as the cottage collapsed in on itself, as Missus and Leafy were swallowed up by the *nothing* he'd unleashed. He'd been so sure he *hadn't* seen her, but her eyes had caught his, in all the swirling dust and darkness, and they'd looked like this girl's.)

'Are you ... ?' he said, and he reached out to take her hand, to

help her to the safety of dry land, but something went wrong and she *almost* took it, and their fingertips brushed and tangled and slipped, and her foot wasn't placed quite right and she tumbled backwards and fell.

Hector shouted her name and Tommo watched helplessly.

She smiled up at him as she fell away.

He couldn't be sure – it happened so quickly, even as it slow-motioned in his head – but he half-believed she winked at him.

*It's happening again*, he thought.

He ran up the path, towards the twittern and a telephone to call for help, leaving Hector in the riverbed with Sascha and her broken arm.

She was older.

She was *their* age.

*Maria was never born.*

(Sascha and Hex, best friends. Ever since they were born, the dynamic duo …)

He almost laughed.

Out of the twittern and into the close, and he ran to Sascha and Jayce's house, hammered on the door.

A teenage boy answered, looking at his phone and with a hand out to collect the post he obviously thought was being delivered.

'It's Sascha,' Tommo said breathlessly, collapsing with his hands on his knees. 'She's fallen off the rope-swing. Broken arm.'

The boy turned and shouted into the house.

'Mum! Call an ambulance!'

And a voice from the kitchen shouted back, 'What, Jay? What did you say?'

And Tommo knew it was him, even though he'd hardly made eye contact and had a stupid haircut now.

And he also knew they weren't and *couldn't* be friends and he shouldn't say anything.

But then, just as Tommo turned to go, message delivered, cavalry on their way, he saw himself turn and say, 'Thank you.'

He meant, *'Thank you for having been my friend in a world you don't remember, when you were someone else entirely.'*

This new, older Jayce looked at him, and said, 'It was fun.'

His eye twinkled and the old smile was there.

And then the tiny moment passed, and a look came over his face as if he were looking at what he'd just said and not recognising it.

*Sometimes the world echoes, bounces once or twice, before it settles,* Tommo thought.

⁂

He felt sad.

He'd been best friends with Jayce as long as he could remember.

There was a hole in his stomach.

But it felt different to being abandoned, to falling out with a friend. The boy he had known no longer existed. It wasn't anyone's fault.

Tommo'd always have the memories, and more memories would pile up in front of them, but that hollowness would remain.

He'd have to be brave.

He'd saved the world.

He thought about Hector and Sascha on the rope-swing.

How he'd once been Hector's best friend, if he believed Maria. (The Maria who only *he* remembered now.) Not *this* Hector, though … but the Hector of the world before last …

He didn't feel sad about that, just curious.

It was a lot.

How many timelines, how many other versions of the world, had there been? Who had been friends with whom? What stories had been told that had been lost forever?

How many throws of the dice did you get?

●

Leaving Sascha and Jayce's house, he had two choices: turn left and go back to the woods, or turn right and head for home.

He opted for the second.

The morning was already late.

He'd been away all night.

Someone might be worried about him.

At the top of the close he paused, wheezing, aching, and pulling his inhaler out of his pocket.

As he took a puff a woman approached.

She wasn't looking where she was going and almost bumped into him.

She was dressed in a dark, but scuffed, suit, and was holding a device in her hand that might've been a mobile phone or might've been something else.

*She is following disturbances set off by last night's Unauthorised Temporal Reweave,* Tommo thought, and smiled at how much like a spy that made him sound.

'Special Agent Jofolofski,' he said.

She stopped and looked at him through her dark glasses.

'Do I know you?' she asked.

I *know you,* he thought.

'I guess not,' he said. 'I just wanted to say … Maria said you tried, and that's all anyone could ask … She wasn't angry …' He paused, gulped air, stumbled the words, felt tears begin to rise, squeezed them back. 'But I'm sorry I couldn't rescue her too. *She* saved *me.*'

The special agent removed her glasses and looked at him.

Her eyes were tired, but not surprised.

'I think we need to talk, don't we?' she said, and handed him her card. 'Call me when you've got yourself cleaned up. You look like you've spent the night fighting the forest.'

'It was worse than that,' he said.

'I'll get the paperwork ready,' she said. 'Unofficial Secrets Act and all that … His Majesty thanks you for your assistance, and so on … and then you can tell me why you're signing it.'

She watched as he walked away, up the road, up the hill.

He could feel her eyes on the back of his neck all the way to the level crossing.

He liked her.

Even in this world, she didn't treat him like a kid.

When he finally turned the corner into his street he saw a police car parked outside his house.

Something inside him whispered, 'Run,' but he didn't listen.

Something else in him whispered, 'Your dad wouldn't care enough to call the police if you went missing, not after one night. Would he?'

Today was today, and the only thing to do with todays is to live them.

*You've lived through all that, seen things no one would believe,* he told himself. *You can do this. Open the door and go home.*

He walked up to the house.

Ran his finger along the white metal of the car as he passed it by.

He'd heard one elderly neighbour leaning in the open door of her house whisper to her husband, 'The missing boy's come home. Told you he weren't really missing.'

She hadn't sounded wholly surprised or impressed.

He wondered if he did this often, in this new world.

The new Tommo, the Tommo he'd have to learn to be.

He passed by the alley, looked up it at the wooden fences, the shadows, the cat lounging on top of a bin.

There was a new car in their drive, a different car to the one in the world before.

(That had to mean something. Would his dad ever really pick a *green* car? Or … ?)

He took a deep breath and walked up the path to his house, went round the back, through the gate, and let his hand rest against the cool metal of the door handle.

The sun above was hot.

He looked like he'd been dragged through a hedge.

The comforting tickle of a wheeze flickered in his throat.

He pressed down on the handle and swung the door open, not knowing what he would find inside. Or who.

And he went in.

# A.F. Harrold

A.F. Harrold is an English poet and author who writes and performs for both children and adults. He is the author of *The Book of Not Entirely Useful Advice*, illustrated by Mini Grey; *The Song from Somewhere Else*, illustrated by Levi Pinfold; the Fizzlebert Stump series, illustrated by Sarah Horne; the Greta Zargo duology, illustrated by Joe Todd-Stanton, and the CILIP Carnegie and Kate Greenaway Medal-longlisted *The Imaginary* and *The Afterwards*, both illustrated by Emily Gravett. He is the anthologist of many poetry collections, including *Midnight Feasts*. He lives in Reading with a stand-up comedian and two cats.

# Levi Pinfold

Levi Pinfold has been drawing from imagination for as long as he can remember. His award-winning picture books include *The Django*, *Black Dog* and *Greenling*. *Black Dog* won the prestigious CILIP Kate Greenaway Medal, and Levi has since been shortlisted twice more for the same award for *The Dam* by David Almond and *The Song from Somewhere Else* by A.F. Harrold, which also won the Amnesty CILIP Honour. Born in the Forest of Dean, Levi now lives with his family in Australia. He likes paintings, books, music and some cats.

# Praise for
# *The Song from Somewhere Else*

'Extraordinary … as moving, strange and profound as David Almond's *Skellig*'

*Guardian*

'Broodingly atmospheric black-and-white illustrations by Levi Pinfold … the tale turns into a fantasy of another world, blending the strange and the everyday'

*Sunday Times*

'Wildly imaginative and heartbreakingly moving … Levi Pinfold's superbly evocative, misty illustrations complete a glorious and unforgettable tale of loyalty, loss and friendship'

*Daily Mail*

'A curious story about two bullied children who end up forming an unlikely friendship based on a haunting melody, an improbable mother, an invasion from another world and a disappearing cat. There are wonderfully evocative pictures by Levi Pinfold'

*Evening Standard*

'What begins as a story of bullying becomes a whirlpool of mystery as Frank tries to undo the damage she has done. A magic story of friendship and love, with atmospheric black-and-white illustrations by Levi Pinfold'

*Irish Examiner*

'There is a delicate sensibility, a happy strangeness, to this; sometimes scary, sometimes funny, always essential. The illustrations by Pinfold – black and white, pencil, dramatic and evocative – are a vital component'

*Big Issue*

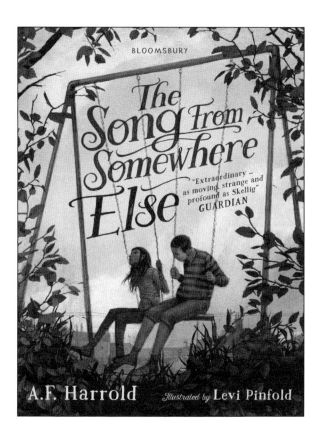

## SOMETIMES YOU FIND FRIENDSHIP WHERE YOU LEAST EXPECT IT.

Longlisted for the CILIP Carnegie Medal
and shortlisted for the Kate Greenaway Medal 2018

Winner of the Amnesty CILIP Honour 2018

# Praise for *The Imaginary*

'By turns scary and funny, touching without being sentimental, and beautifully illustrated by Emily Gravett, *The Imaginary* is a delight from start to finish'

*Financial Times*

'A moving read about loyalty and belief in the extraordinary'

*Guardian*

'The kind of children's book that's the reason why adults should never stop reading children's books. Touching, exciting and wonderful to look at (Emily Gravett's illustrations are incredible), I absolutely adored this. And I cried a little bit'

Robin Stevens

'A glorious delight … Loved it!'

Jeremy Strong

'Packed full of heart'

Phil Earle, *Guardian*

'This is young fiction of the very best quality, showcasing inspiration, inventiveness and an intoxicating passion for storytelling. *The Imaginary* has the potential to be a family favourite and a future classic'

BookTrust

'A richly visualised story which explores imaginary friends and the very special role they play in children's lives. Emily Gravett's illustrations capture the hazy world of the imaginaries brilliantly'

Julia Eccleshare, Lovereading4kids

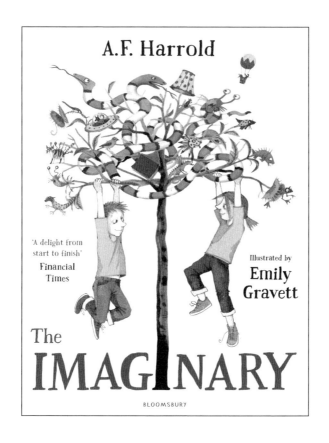

A.F. Harrold

'A delight from start to finish'
**Financial Times**

Illustrated by
**Emily Gravett**

The
# IMAGINARY

BLOOMSBURY

RUDGER IS AMANDA'S BEST FRIEND.

HE DOESN'T EXIST.

BUT NOBODY'S PERFECT.

Winner of the UKLA 2016 Book Award in the 7–11 category

Longlisted for the CILIP Carnegie Medal
and the Kate Greenaway Medal 2016

# Praise for The Afterwards

'A brave, challenging and beautifully written book that unflinchingly confronts death, grief and denial, but which is redeemed by a dark humour and, beneath everything, a beating heart of love. Young readers will root for the compelling character of Ember and, when she's faced with an agonising decision, will urge her to choose life'

*Daily Mail*

'An extraordinary book. This is a meditative, unsettling, tender exploration of what might happen after death'

*Guardian*

'A moving, thoughtful tale of friendship, loss and learning to grieve, beautifully complemented with illustrations by Emily Gravett'

*WRD* magazine

'Beautifully written by a wordsmith of great skill ... tenderness and compassion flows from every page even though this story is not afraid to be sad and scary or even, at times, darkly funny. It's a book about love and facing up to loss, and it's profoundly moving'

The Bookbag

'Poignant and thought-provoking ... It's a story that will make you think and certainly reflect on life. Consider it as a train ride into the reader's past, and when the last page has been turned, a journey into the reader's future. A brilliant and much recommended read'

Mr Ripley's Enchanted Books

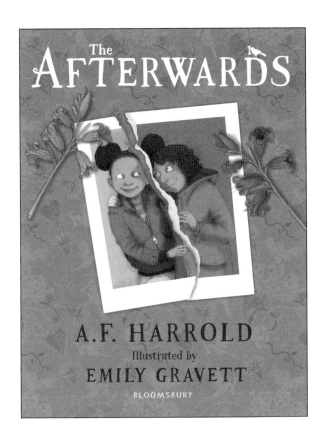

EMBER AND NESS ARE BEST FRIENDS.
NOTHING CHANGES THAT.

A powerful, poignant, darkly comic and deeply moving
story about friendship at its most extraordinary.
Perfect for fans of Neil Gaiman.

LOOK OUT FOR THIS RIOTOUS
CELEBRATION OF WORDS AND A MODERN
TAKE ON CAUTIONARY TALES

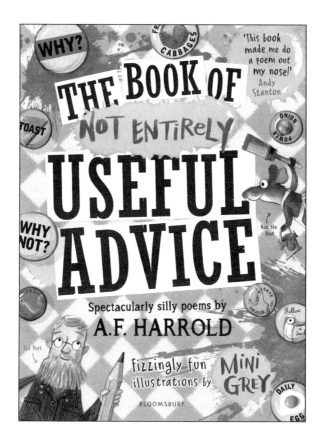

Featuring advice on parrots, gravy, mathematics, castles
(bouncy), spiders, vegetables (various), breakfast,
cakes, and removing ducks from soup.

LOOK OUT FOR

THIS SCRUMPTIOUS POETRY

COLLECTION

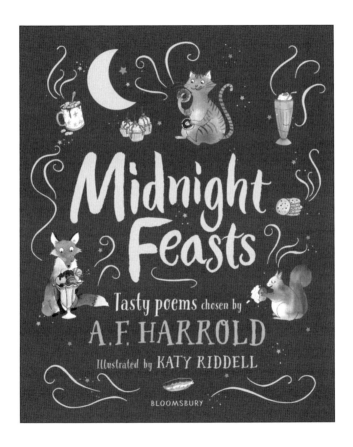

From chocolate, rice pudding and sandwiches to breakfast in
bed, marmalade in the bath and the fruit of a mythical jelabi
tree, this delicious collection of poems will delight and
tickle your taste buds.

GRETA ZARGO DOESN'T KNOW IT,
BUT SHE IS ABOUT TO SAVE
THE WORLD!

'A child-friendly *The Hitchhiker's Guide to the Galaxy* mash-up with
*The Great British Bake Off* … a hilariously silly joy of a book'
BookTrust

GRETA ZARGO DOESN'T KNOW IT,
BUT SHE IS ABOUT TO SAVE
THE WORLD – AGAIN!

'Delicious for its wit'
*Sunday Times*

# DISCOVER ALL
# FIZZLEBERT STUMP'S
# ADVENTURES

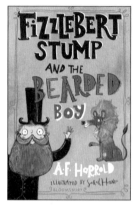

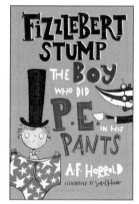